THE FINAL LESSON

THE FINAL LESSON

Janelle R. Wols

iUniverse, Inc.
New York   Bloomington

The Final Lesson

This is a work of fiction. All of the characters, names, incidents,
organizations, and dialogue in this novel are either the products
of the author's imagination or are used fictitiously.

iUniverse books may be ordered through booksellers or by contacting:

iUniverse
1663 Liberty Drive
Bloomington, IN 47403
www.iuniverse.com
1-800-Authors (1-800-288-4677)

Because of the dynamic nature of the Internet, any Web addresses or
links contained in this book may have changed since publication and
may no longer be valid. The views expressed in this work are solely those
of the author and do not necessarily reflect the views of the publisher, and
the publisher hereby disclaims any responsibility for them.

ISBN: 978-1-4401-3136-3 (sc)
ISBN: 978-1-4401-3137-0 (ebook)

Printed in the United States of America

iUniverse rev. date: 04/28/2009

For my husband, Sam Wols,
for every journey we take in life,

I am grateful to be sharing it with someone
as wonderful as you, I love you.

CHAPTER ONE
The Last Victim

———————— ◊ ————————

The local police were waiting for the FBI agents to show up at the crime scene. Upon arriving at the scene the agents asked them who was in charge and were sent to the local homicide detective originally assigned to the case. The homicide detective had contacted the Federal Bureau of Investigations when he realized that the homicide fit the description of other killings in a neighboring state, and because the killings had crossed state lines it fell under FBI jurisdiction. The FBI agents asked the detective for the details of the case. Once the detective shared the information that he learned from the witnesses and family the FBI agents knew it was a match for the other killings. This was the fourth killing and the agents believed they were looking for a serial killer.

The victim was young and female, barely 18 years of age. She went out to a movie with friends and never made it home according to her parents. They reported her missing over a month ago. The assumption by the local officials was that she had probably run away with a boyfriend. The body was found in a new housing development, in a home that was in the middle of construction. The construction workers found the body when they arrived on site for work that morning. There was no way of telling how long the body had been there. The construction workers had not been at this site in over two months. They would complete one section of the house and move on to the next house to complete the same section. They continued through the development doing this before returning to the start and beginning the next stage. Fall had begun and the rain started to fall a few months before and that limited the number of days that they could work causing the production of the homes to slow. This house had the frame and most of the exterior walls up. This prevented anyone from seeing into the home and calling in the body earlier.

There was no visual sign of the cause of death although the body had bruising and many other marks. There were marks on her wrist and ankles, as well as around her waist, bruising and chaffing from rope presumably. It appeared that she had been tied up but there was no sign of strangulation, deep cuts, or any other wounds to cause her death. There was not a blow to the head that they could find or any wounds, bruising, or blood on the head. This only confirmed the original assumption that this murder followed the same modus operandi, or M.O. as the others. They knew that the medical examiner would find that this girl died from either starvation or hypothermia. The M.E. had not been able to ascertain with the other victims whether they died from the starvation or the hypothermia. Since both were present the M.E. could not be positive which would have been the initial cause of death. In the case of this victim the same question held true. The body may have turned blue in color after being dumped at the site where it was found. There were signs of starvation and the skin was starting to hang lazily on the victim. The M.E. would have to conduct the autopsy before they could know more.

The FBI agents knew what the M.E. would find in the autopsy so they decided to move ahead with the investigation. The lead agent was Calvin Fisher, but his team called him Fish. He was the senior agent and had been with the FBI for almost twenty years. He had worked cases on serial killers before and felt that the key to catching them was to understand them. That is where Agent Rhonda Carr comes in; she was a behavioral specialist whose job was to give a description of the killer based on the clues established from each victim and where they were found. For the last seven years she has worked closely with Fisher and they made a good team. When she first joined the team Fisher felt that she was too much of a bookworm to be a field agent. It was only a short time before she proved that she could hold her own in the field. She was trained in martial arts and always thought on her feet. She could think out a situation and the possibilities before the situation was upon her. Fisher trusted her input in the field and in the office because she was good at her job. He went to her first to find out what she thought about the killer.

"Have you reviewed the information that has been passed on to us so far about this case?" Fisher asks Carr.

"I have. There are a couple of things that I am unsure of here. There is no sexuality in these crimes so I cannot be positive that the person we are looking for is male. However, I believe we are looking for a male and assume that this is the killer's way of acting out his hate of women. He was probably abused as a child by a woman, or perhaps it is just a power thing for him," Carr answers.

"So an abused child turned into a man who hates women that is seeking the feeling of power. Well, that won't be hard to find," Fisher answers sarcastically.

"Well, he wants the women to suffer; he preys on young females so perhaps he has an attraction to this type of woman and wants them to pay for what happened to him. The question is whether or not he watches them suffer or if he is just dropping them somewhere and leaving them there. If he stays then he is getting some sort of feeling from it, probably excitement, from watching them die. However, if he just leaves them behind to let them die alone, then he may be acting out his own abandonment issues," Carr elaborates.

"So, we need more information is what you are telling me?"

"Yes, we will have to review the cases and see what clues jump out at us," Carr states matter-of-factly.

"Get to it then." Fisher moves away from Carr and heads towards his other agents to give them their direction.

Fisher approached the other three agents standing in a circle talking about the case; they are part of Fisher's team. The agent speaking as Fisher walked up was Agent Chris Dalton, the muscle of the team. Dalton was an ex-marine who was trained in Special Forces and he was the enforcer for the team. He was talking about the frequency of the killings with his two teammates, Agent Benjamin Burke and Agent Greg Vickers. Agent Burke was a new addition to the team and the youngest in the group. He was the "kid" in the group and was often called "kid" as a nickname, his young age and technical experience made him an appreciated asset to the team. Fisher's team did not use many of the new technological advances until Burke came along. He did all the computer work and offered all the analysis of the new systems offered by the FBI. Agent Greg Vickers was older than Burke but was not far behind in understanding the new technologies. However, he had more field experience so he became the middleman for those on the team who were older and did not utilize the technology and the new younger member who felt that the technology was essential to every case. The conversation continued for a few minutes before Fisher interjected.

"So we think this killer is on a time table?" Fisher muses over the conversation.

"He is traveling at a very fast pace, he kills a few in one area before moving on to another. From the bodies that we have found it seems that he is killing every two to three weeks. His time pattern has not changed," Vickers offers to Fisher.

"He seems to wait until one victim is dead before moving on to another, however there is almost no time between when he takes one and another which makes me think that he is not waiting and watching but using any opportunity that appears before him. A case of wrong place and wrong time for the victim," Burke adds quickly.

"What do you think, Carr?" Dalton asks as she approaches the group.

"I think he could be leaving the victims and searching out a new one in the area before the victim has died, presuming they have all been taken and left at the site we found them," Carr answers. "It appears by staying in the area he wants to see them die, so I would assume that he is not only finding his next victim while one dies but returning to the location to check that the first victim is dead. Also, he must be spending some time finding the appropriate locations so that they are not found too soon."

"We will have to look more into the first three victims to find more patterns," Burke states already making notes in his head.

"Then that will be your job, kid," Fisher says pointing at him.

"I will assist him in analyzing the commonalities for all the victims," Vickers offers.

"Fine. Dalton you get out in the field and see what you can find out from witnesses, people who were with the victims before they went missing. Maybe someone saw something and did not realize they saw it. Carr, you see if you can get me some sort of idea on where this guy will show up next or how he is picking these girls," Fisher had barked out the orders and everyone dispersed.

Carr arrived back at the office and began searching through the case looking for something that would let her into the killer's mind. She worked tediously for hours wanting something to pop out at her. After hours of no substantial clues she decided to take a break and let her mind rest for a moment. She felt that perhaps she was missing something in her own frustration. She decided to check in with the medical examiner and find out if there was anything new the body could tell her. She called Fisher and let him know that she was heading to see the M.E. and he decided to meet her there.

By the time that Carr arrived at the medical examiner's

office she already felt fresher and more alert than when she originally took the break. Fisher was there at the door waiting for her. They entered together walking directly into the autopsy room. The examiner was just finishing up, but warned them upon entering that there were some answers he did not have yet. The first question they asked the M.E. was the cause of death. He explained to them that the liver had begun to break down as well as the muscle tissue in the body, signs that the victim suffered from starvation. The victim's lips and ears had become blue as well as some of her extremities like her fingers and toes, suggesting hypothermia. The overall look of the skin on the victim was loose but pale and puffy. Other major organs had started to fail but the official cause of death was cardiac arrest, the cause of the heart stopping could have been due to the starvation or the hypothermia, both were present and both left untreated would have caused the heart to fail. The medical examiner found what the Agents knew that he would. There were no surprises, the previous victims had the same report.

"And the tox screen? Were there any toxins in the victims system?" Fisher asks.

"I do not have the reports yet, but I sent the blood work and all other tests out for analysis. However, I did find one new thing on this victim. The victim had chewed up the inside of her bottom lip, and if there was some type of drug or something put into her mouth it would have made it into her blood stream through the open wound in her mouth. I sent tissue samples out for testing in case she had any oral contact with the killer."

"Ok, thank you. Please let us know as soon as you find something." Fisher took Carr by the arm and they left to continue the investigation.

CHAPTER TWO
Friday

———— ◊ ————

The bell rings and all of the students file into the classroom, talking and sitting next to their friends. It was like any other Friday, everyone was talking about their plans for the upcoming weekend; who was having parties, whose parents were out of town, and who was hooking up with whom. The day is almost over, two more classes and school is out for the day. The teacher spends the next few minutes trying to settle the students and take roll. Although she is not paying much attention, this is Nicole's favorite class. It is an elective, an art class. She loves art, although her parents often wish that she would spend as much time on her other studies as she does painting.

Nicole is a senior in high school and loves being in

high school. She is part of the Drama Club, gets to work on her art at school, and is dating one of the lead scorers on the basketball team. She has several good friends but one best friend, whom she has known since elementary school. This best friend and a few of the other close friends are also in the art class with her. She takes the class to work on her art and learn about other artists, while her friends take the class to have a full class period of gossip. The teacher allows the students to develop their creativity on their own and some of the students like to take advantage of that kind of teaching. They use the class as a free period to socialize. Nicole has been able to find a happy medium and is able to talk and gossip while painting. She has two of her favorite things in life together for an hour out of every school day. She starts to arrange her painting materials while she discusses with her friends the plans for the weekend. Her best friend Jillian urging her to come to a party on Saturday night that one of the basketball players is having at his house.

"Whose party is it?" Nicole asks.

"It is Jay's party. His parents are going to Cabo for the weekend and he is having everyone over."

"So what's the deal? What kind of party is it?" Nicole probes further into the gossip about the party.

"Just everyone hanging out, his older brother is going to supply the drinks for everyone. Everyone is going to be there."

"Who is everyone?"

"Everyone. Including your man, so you better go, Alicia is going to be there and you know what she will do if you are not there," Jillian says giving Nicole a serious look.

"I trust Justin. He wouldn't do anything to hurt me." Nicole states with a smile.

Nicole and Justin have been dating since freshman year and Nicole knows that Justin may be a jock, but that he loves her and would not cheat on her. Justin may act like a jerk sometimes when he is with his friends but he always considers how she feels and is there for her in the end. Alicia on the other hand is the typical two-faced bitch that most girls meet in high school. Alicia is so unhappy with herself and her life that she is always trying to make everyone else miserable like her. She likes Justin, as many other girls do, but she has made it her personal goal to separate Nicole from Justin. Alicia is jealous of Nicole for many reasons, not just her boyfriend.

Nicole has good friends and is beautiful. Nicole has classic good looks with a nice body with a larger chest than most of the other seventeen-year-old girls. She has long brown wavy hair, gorgeous green eyes, high cheekbones, and big pouty lips. Nicole hates Alicia but sometimes she feels sorry for her too. Alicia is a normal teenager, with a small acne problem. She has short brown hair and brown eyes. She has a small well-shaped figure with long thin legs. Alicia's body is more like a runway model than a Marilyn Monroe. Jillian is always there to remind Nicole that Alicia is a problem even though Nicole would often rather forget about her. Nicole also knows that Jillian is right, there will be a lot of drama and gossip if she does not go to the party and Alicia and Justin are both there.

"Yeah, but you know she will get wasted and throw herself at him," Jillian points out backing up her argument.

"Well, I guess I am going then. Who else is going?" Nicole asks.

"Good," Jillian states with a smile. "You know that new girl is telling everyone that she is coming with an older guy. The guy is supposedly 22 years old and according to what she is telling people he is supposed to be hot."

"Do you think she will show up?" Nicole jokes back with a smile.

"Last time she talked about coming to a party with some guy from a band and never showed up … you tell me."

"Hey, but I saw her get dropped off to school by a guy that was very hot," Adria joins the conversation.

"Yeah, but that could have been her brother or something," Sarah points out with a laugh.

"Well, we will see tomorrow," Nicole states with a little laugh.

"Is Cameron coming?" Sarah is directing this question to Jillian.

"He is going to try. He works late but he is going

to try to get off work early and come by." Cameron is Jillian's boyfriend that graduated the year before.

"So what time are we heading over?" Nicole asks.

"Jay said like six or seven. His parents leave tonight but he works in the morning. He said he will be home around three and his brother will be there with drinks around five," Adria answers.

"So I am telling my parents that I am staying at Jillian's, how about you two?" Nicole asks Adria and Sarah, to be sure they all have their stories straight.

"We can say the same. I will tell my parents we are having a slumber party, like a girl's movie night or something." Sarah and Adria nod in agreement.

The girls spend the rest of the class period talking about the party and how excited they all are. Adria and Sarah are two peas in a pod. They could be sisters they look so much alike. They also act alike, making them appear even more like sisters. Adria is tall and pretty, wearing strategically placed clothing to show off her nice features and hide what she feels are her flaws, like her very large behind. Sarah is the opposite, she likes to show off her rear end in tight jeans and hide that she is not as developed in the chest area. They both have blonde hair, blue eyes, and a light complexion.

Jillian is the fiery part of the group. She has brown hair with red throughout and large round blue eyes. She has a sporty figure that makes any outfit look good and has the attitude to match any style that she wears. She has been dating Cameron since the beginning of her junior year. He is a year older and attending the local junior college. She likes having a boyfriend that is somewhat separate from the drama at school, but she also likes that everyone knows him and that although many other girls like him, he has chosen to love her.

There is only five minutes of class left so the girls all begin to pack up their things and wait for the bell to ring for passing period. Once the bell rings they all file through the door and walk to their lockers. Nicole grabs her history book for the next class and walks to meet Justin at his locker. She beat him to the locker so she leans against the lockers waiting for him. He walks up only moments later saying hello with a kiss, as he pulls her away from the locker with one arm around her waist. She begins questioning him about the party the next day and what the plan will be. Justin is tall and strong, with brown hair. He has big brown eyes with long dark lashes combined with a smile that makes you smile just to think about it. He dresses and walks like a jock, but he is not careless with his studies, he has good grades and studies hard.

"Are we going to the party at Jay's tomorrow?" Nicole asks wiggling out of his arm playfully.

"You mean you already decided that we are going to the party," Justin says with a smile and a raised eyebrow.

"Well, everyone is going to be there, and I heard

you already told Jay you were going to be there," Nicole challenges him.

"Let me guess, the three musketeers said that. I told Jay I would see. That is not the same thing, but it should be fun." He smiles at his own nickname for Jillian, Adria, and Sarah.

"Well, I could always go without you …" the warning bell interrupts Nicole's joking.

"Gotta go. See you after school babe," Justin kisses Nicole quickly and they both are off and on their way to class.

Nicole arrives at her next class and sits down. She does not like her history class because she cannot seem to get her head around it. There are too many things to memorize and it is hard to remember things that do not amuse you. She always remembers her art history because she loves art but actual world history is a different story. She does not have the girls in this class with her but she does talk with another friend that she sits with, Aaron. He is what everyone calls a geek, but she thinks that he is incredibly nice and smart. She likes talking to him, although she only does so in class. Aaron never seems to mind though; she is always nice to him and that is all he asks for. Aaron is a small guy, glasses, and uncontrollable curly black hair. He is the type of guy that Nicole's mom always says will be attractive when he gets older, when all the jocks will become bald and fat. That is a nice thought but to Nicole and all the other girls at the school all that matters is how the guys look now and what the other people at school will say about them. Class starts and Nicole and Aaron complain together about the subject, although Nicole knows that Aaron probably really enjoys the subject and is only complaining with her to make her feel better.

"I have good news," Aaron whispers to Nicole.

"What's up?" She whispers back.

"I got accepted …" There is a pause in his voice as Nicole turns to face him.

"To Stanford." His face lights up in an ear-to-ear grin as he says this.

"Really?" She smiles back with genuine excitement for him.

"Yeah, I am going to the west coast … away from everyone here and the cold." Aaron is speaking in a hushed voice but a little loudly he realizes as he receives a strict glare from the teacher that means stop talking. Nicole knows how happy he is about moving away from all the people that they go to school with and she is happy for him. They remain quiet until the end of the period. As they walk out of class she offers him a warm congratulations and a hug. She is proud of him and happy that his dreams are coming true. However, it does make her wonder about her own college applications, since she has not heard yet.

The end of the school day comes quickly and Nicole goes to her locker where she meets up with her friends.

Jillian is ready to go home but decides to hang out with her friends while Nicole goes to Drama Club. They are practicing for an upcoming play, a modern remake of Romeo and Juliet. It was rewritten by one of the students in Drama Club, and Nicole is to play Juliet to the not yet cast Romeo. They will be doing auditions for the part of Romeo today and the girls thought they would hang out and see who will be playing the part opposite their friend. There are numerous guys trying out for the part but most of them are horrible. They are so bad in most cases that it is hysterical. The bloopers of the auditions could be a play by itself.

The first person to try out is a shy guy that the girls do not recognize and he blunders over the lines while repeating himself continually. When he steps forward to go onto one knee he falls one foot over the other and lands on his head. He is excused and walks away rubbing his forehead. The second guy to try is a little better with the words but is very awkward in his movement. He is both extremely tall and very skinny. His arms flail in circles around his small head as if he is dancing with every word he says. It is quite funny to watch, and too overdramatic for the part. The third guy to try is not half bad at the acting part. However, everyone who was watching knew he was a failing student. In order to be a part of any extracurricular activity you have to have a minimum grade point average of 2.5. They all knew that this guy did not have that. The fourth and fifth guys are not bad but not as great as a Romeo should be either. By the time the sixth guy comes onto stage to audition pretty much everyone has given up on finding the right person for Romeo.

The sixth guy to try out is a cute guy that all the girls know, but did not know that he had any interest in acting or plays. He begins and they all know right away that he is the perfect Romeo and instantly Adria and Sarah both have crushes. He practically sings through the lines with an authority in his voice that catches everyone's attention. His astonishing performance does not stop at a beautiful read of the script as he also moves gracefully with every word. Nicole knows right away that this is the person that will play Romeo to her Juliet. Once they offer him the part the day's work is all done. It is time to go home and the girls all gather to leave together. Nicole promises to call Jillian after she talks to her parents about staying the night and let her know the plan for Saturday. Nicole settles into the car and checks her phone, Justin has sent her a text message that he is thinking about her and will see her at the game tonight. She puts her phone down and heads home.

CHAPTER THREE
Parents

————————— ◊ —————————

Nicole lives close to the high school and makes it home quickly. When she enters the house she hears arguing. Her parents are in the kitchen and practically yelling at each other, so they do not hear her come in. She starts towards the kitchen but decides to head straight upstairs and not let them know that she is home. Once she reaches upstairs she closes her bedroom door but not before hearing her name from downstairs. She realizes that they are arguing about her and she is not sure why. She sits on her bed wondering what she has done or what they may have caught her for. She cannot think of anything recently that may be causing them to argue. She is debating in her mind whether or not to head downstairs and suffer the firing range or to just hide out. It is getting late though and she does not want to miss the beginning of Justin's game tonight. She takes a few deep breaths and stands to go downstairs. Halfway down the stairs she hears why they are arguing and she hesitates, she is not ready for this battle. She decides to continue and enters the kitchen, for a moment it is quiet and then her mother starts.

"What the hell were you thinking?" She says with a quivering voice trying not to yell.

"What she means is why didn't you discuss this with us?" Nicole's dad interrupts trying to keep the conversation calm. This statement earns him a menacing look from Nicole's mother.

"We had an agreement that you would keep up your studies if we let you take some art classes and then you make these kinds of decisions without even talking to us?" Nicole's mom was almost whining now.

"Mom. I just wanted to see ..." Nicole starts to respond to the questioning.

"See what? You are going to state and getting a degree," her mother interrupts.

"But if I got in then my portfolio was good enough and ..." She is interrupted again.

"We know you are talented Hun, it is just that the avenue we discussed was not an art school. It was a degree that you can fall back on in the real world," her father explains.

"You both have fallen out of the real world. Art is

going to take her nowhere and she is getting a degree. That is it!" Her mother yells.

"No! I am not, Mom. If I got in then I am going. I want to work on my art," Nicole shouts back at her mother.

"This is all your fault! You encouraged her ..." Nicole's mom throws a look at her husband as she accuses him.

"Mom! I did it on my own. I prepared a portfolio with my art teacher and I sent it to the school and I filled out the application. It is a hard school to get into and if I got in," Nicole is trying to make her mom understand that it is worth celebrating not fighting.

"I don't want to hear anymore. We will talk more later, once everyone has calmed down," her father says looking at Nicole with a look that tells her to leave the room.

"But I was going to go to Justin's game. ..." Nicole ventures and her mother throws her arms into the air.

"Go. Give your mom a chance to calm down and we will talk in the morning. Ten o'clock tonight no later." Nicole's dad ushers her out of the room.

Nicole does not want to push her luck any more than she already has so she gets her things and leaves. She walks out to her car, gets in, and takes a deep breath. Then she laughs and with butterflies in her stomach and a big smile on her face she starts to drive. She can not believe it but she got in. She got into the toughest art academy in the area. She can not wait to tell Justin and Jillian so she speeds off towards the school for the game. There is nothing in the world that she wants more than to pursue her art. They will be happy for her and maybe they can celebrate at the party tomorrow. She arrives at the game and pays for her ticket in. She finds Jillian quickly in the stands and climbs the steps to sit with her. She wants to tell her the news right away, but she wants to tell Justin also, so she has to wait until the game is over.

It is the end of the first quarter when Nicole arrives. Justin watches her climb into the stands while he is in the huddle with the coach. He smiles up at her not sure if she sees him or not. She notices the smile and she makes a little wave while sitting down next to Jillian. She remembers the first time she saw Justin play basketball. He has changed some from freshman year but the way he looks in his uniform, with the sweat glistening on his toned shoulders and arms, still excites her. She watches the game intently she likes discussing the game with her man after the game ends. This keeps her in the loop with the players and Justin's friends when the team goes out to eat after each game. Still she is excited about her own news and watches the clock closely hoping that it will move faster. It seems like forever to her but the game ends and she and Jillian head out to the parking lot where they will meet Justin after the coach is finished talking to the team and they shower and change.

Nicole is talking to Jillian with her back turned when Justin sneaks up from behind grabbing Nicole's waist and lifting her into the air. Nicole shrieks for him to let her down while giggling. Justin turns her around in the air to face him and brings her down slightly, kissing her before allowing her to touch the ground. Once back on the ground she tells him to stop playing and that she has some news. They both look at her waiting for her to continue.

"I got into the Art Academy," Nicole leaves it hanging in the air for a moment.

"Are you kidding?" Jillian asks.

"Really babe? That is great! Did you tell your parents?" Justin says with a sour face.

"Yeah, they got the mail before I did," Nicole shakes her head as if to say that is bad.

"What did they say?"

"That I can't go. My mom says I have to get a, quote, real degree. My dad seems stuck in the middle," Nicole says making quotation marks in the air.

"What are you going to do?" Justin seems very interested in the answer.

"I don't know. I want to follow my art not go to state. I don't want to fight with my parents the rest of the year though either. I hoped they would be more understanding," Nicole explains.

"How are you here and not at home fighting with the rents?" Jillian questions.

"Dad sent me out for cool off time," Nicole again makes finger quotes in the air as she says this.

"So what about the party tomorrow? Did you ask to stay at my house?" Jillian knows that she did not ask.

"It was not the right time. I will ask in the morning after they have calmed down. Maybe I will act like I am considering state to make them happy and save the fight for later, I don't know. I don't understand why they can't let me live my own life. It is my life after all. It is like they don't know what it is like to love something and want to do it all the time. All they ever talk about is how I can not make money painting. It is not about money … they just don't understand," Nicole is starting to vent.

"And they probably never will. I understand that you need to be at the party tomorrow though. I told Jay I would be there after you said we were going. I don't want to deal with the crap if you are not there with me," Justin is changing the subject back to the party to avoid an "I hate my parents" conversation. Although he is pretty sure he could win.

"You know I don't think my parents have ever asked me what I want to do or be. They just tell me what to do. They don't pay much attention to things I like either. They usually only comment on things I like if they are saying how much they don't like it. Like the TV shows I watch and my music and well everything about me it seems," Jillian has not even heard Justin talking and has started to complain about her parents too.

"I know. Mine too. They don't try to enjoy the stuff with me. It is always about when they were my age or how they think that they understand because they have been there. They don't realize how much different it is now," Nicole is ignoring Justin also and not allowing the topic to be changed.

"You know your parents are just worried that if you don't get a degree that you will have trouble with jobs later," Justin is switching strategies and defending the parents.

"I will have a degree. An art degree."

"I know but your parents are probably thinking more like a business degree or something. I love your art and I am proud of you for getting into such a hard school. I just don't want to spend all night arguing about our parents," Justin is trying to justify his defending the parents.

"He is right. We need to be celebrating! You got into your art school and Justin won tonight and tomorrow we have an awesome party to attend." Quickly raising the spirits Jillian directs them to the cars.

"I have to be home by ten so we do not have much time. If I am going to go to the party tomorrow I need to keep my dad on my side," Nicole says moving towards her own car.

"Alright then. I will talk to you tomorrow. Call me and let me know how everything goes," with a kiss Justin leaves and Jillian and Nicole are left alone.

"You will call me tomorrow and let me know what they say about the party right?" Jillian asks.

"Of course. I will talk to you as soon as I finish talking to my parents," Nicole answers.

"Alright, cuz you have to go to this party. Everyone will be there."

"I will. Talk to you tomorrow," Nicole says as she sits into her car to leave.

Nicole does not want to go home because she is afraid that her parents are still fighting. She is more afraid however of being late and getting into trouble for that. She arrives home in plenty of time for the 10pm curfew that her father assigned her when she left. The house is quiet when she comes in so she sneaks up to her room. Once in her room she sends Jillian and Justin both a text message that she made it home and that there is no bad news yet. Jillian answers that she is out grabbing a bite to eat with Adria and Sarah. She adds that they both say "Congratulations" for getting into art school. This makes Nicole smile and she remembers why she is fighting with her parents to go to art school. She takes out a sketch pad and starts drawing some pictures that she took in her mind that night while at the basketball game. Before too long has past she realizes that she has not received a text message back from Justin so she messages him again asking what's up. A while passes before he responds that he is at home and going to bed so goodnight. This delay makes Nicole worry that he may be out with other girls and does not want to tell her or let them know that he is still taken. She is probably just being paranoid but just in case she has to go to the party tomorrow night.

CHAPTER FOUR
Saturday

———— ◊ ————

Nicole wakes up late on Saturday and goes downstairs. She pours a bowl of cereal as her mother enters the kitchen for another cup of coffee. They look at each other without saying anything at first then they both mutter a hello. Moments pass and her father enters the kitchen also. She knows this means that the conversation is about to take place since they both are in the kitchen with her. She sits quietly awaiting her fate. Her mother and father are staring at each other as if trying to force one another to speak first. Nicole is not tempted to interrupt this staring match and waits for one of them to start. Her father takes the lead and begins.

"Your mother and I want you to understand that we want what is best for you. It may seem like we are being mean or telling you to do only what we want you to but that is not the case. We love that you have a talent for art but we want to be sure that you have an education to fall back on in life. We feel that even with a talent in art there are not many jobs out there that you can do to pay the rent. We think that if you want to continue painting and such that is fine, even if you want to make a job out of it. We just want to be sure that if you stray from the art or you decide it is not a job that you want to do that you have a back up plan. Something to pay the bills while you practice your art," her father is running out of steam staring at Nicole who is showing no response.

"We want to know that you can take care of yourself. If you go to state you can still take art classes but continue your general education also. We are not saying that you can not make it with your art, you may be able to. We just don't want you to put all your eggs in one basket," her mother is wrapping up the speech and waiting for a response from Nicole.

"I know that you want me to have a good job and all but I love my art and I want my job to be something I love to do. What I love to do is art. I love to sketch and paint and that is what I want to do," Nicole states simply.

"And what job are you going to work in order to do that. You need money to open a gallery of your work. You also need an agent and a publicist to get people to look at your art oh and no one will pay much for your pieces if your name is not known. Most of the paintings that sell for a lot of money sell best after the painter has developed a name or is dead. So what kind of job were you planning on?" Nicole can tell her mother is getting angry.

"I understand all of that but at the art academy I can meet the right people to move in the gallery circles or I may learn computer art and work for a company like Disney making animated films. I am not sure which actual job I want yet but I want the chance to explore my options with art. Can't you understand that? I can always go back to state if I need to but I may not ever get another chance at an art academy like the one I got into. It's a big deal!" Nicole feels like she is beating her head against a wall.

"We do understand that you have dreams and we want you to follow them. It is just that many people say they will do college later and they never do. We do not want you to be one of those people," her mom is trying to explain it the best way she can to her daughter.

"You don't get it. The art academy is college and a great opportunity and I am going." Nicole is getting mad and finishes this statement with her arms folded across her chest.

"You will do what we say you will do. You still live under our roof and we say you are going to state," her mom is equally angry.

"Now, maybe we can come to some compromise but for now let's just focus on you finishing high school and we will work on the rest later," her father is right; there is no point in continuing this argument at this time.

"Fine we can continue this later. Nicole you really need to think about your future. I know how talented you are but I worry about you," Mom is calming down already.

"I know. Maybe I could look into some of the jobs I could do with my art and an education from the art academy and then we could go over them together," Nicole offers following her fathers lead to compromise.

"Alright then we will revisit the subject later when both sides can offer more material and information. In the future honey, please come to us before you make a decision like this and we find out through the mail."

"That is the worst part Nicole, it is like you were lying to us the whole time," her mom is not ready to abandon the fight.

"I know. I am sorry," Nicole says with her head down.

"Alright," Mom and Dad say in unison.

Nicole waits a moment before venturing to ask about staying at Jillian's for the night. She is a little hesitant because of the fighting but she knows if she waits until later that they will say no, that she should have asked them earlier.

"Mom, I wanted to ask you if I could stay at Jillian's house tonight. The girls and I were going to get together, go to a movie and stay the night at Jillian's. You know, a girls night," she lets the end of the sentence hang in the air.

"Are you kidding?" Mom says with wide eyes.

"Honey, why don't you stay in tonight," her dad adds.

"I don't see what the problem is. Besides I already told the girls I would go."

"But we did not tell *you* that you could go," her dad seems to be getting angry now, she knows she should stop pushing the issue but she continues on.

"Because I do something good ... like get into a school that others can't ... I should be punished?" Nicole is not backing down.

"No. Because you lied you will be punished. You will stay in all weekend. That's final," Dad states.

"What?" She says throwing her arms dramatically into the air.

"You heard your father."

"Fine. You win," she directs at her Mom and heads up to her room. Half way up the stairs she turns and yells, "You're only happy if I'm miserable!"

Her parents look at each other shaking their heads they try to remember what it is like to be a teenager when they deal with Nicole but sometimes Nicole makes it very hard to do. Nicole is already in her room with her paints out. She begins painting while she devises her exit strategy for the evening. She is painting a large glass door with adjacent glass windows. Through the doors she paints walls with color, she is making paintings within her painting. She is creating a gallery, one like she hopes to own. She paints quietly waiting for the hours to go by once her parents fall asleep she will leave and head over to the party.

They go to bed early and shut the bedroom door. Nicole knows that does not mean that they are going to sleep but that they are going to talk. She knows they are probably talking about her. She decides to wait for an hour or two before attempting to sneak out of the house. She sends a text message to Jill that she will be on her way in an hour or two and that she will meet her at Jay's house. She does not want to chance her parents hearing a car pull up or her car leaving so she will walk to his house. It will take only a short time to walk to Jay's house, maybe half an hour tops. It will be nice to walk out under the stars even if it is very cold outside. She starts to get dressed for the party making sure to wear a warm coat. It will be freezing on the way home in the early morning so she will probably have Justin drive her home but only to the end of the block and then she will walk, so she will want to be warm.

Once she is sure it is safe she tiptoes downstairs making sure to step along one corner of each step to prevent squeaking. Her heart is pacing very quickly with the thought that she may get caught. She then goes out the sliding glass door into the backyard, leaving the sliding door unlocked for her return in the morning. She leaves a pair of sweats and a long t-shirt just inside the door to change into upon her return, in case her parents catch her coming back into the house. She then leaves through the gate at the side of the house and walks out to the sidewalk. Her heart starts to slow and she starts to walk to the party. It is cold out so she tightens her coat and folds her arms across her chest. She quickens her pace to try to keep warm. It takes her approximately a half hour to walk to Jay's house just as she thought it would and she smiles as she walks up to the house knowing that it will be warm inside.

She rings the bell and one of the guys from the basketball team opens the door. She smiles and he waves her in. She immediately walks towards the kitchen where she knows her man will be, with the rest of the guys drinking and making jokes. She enters the kitchen to see her enemy Alicia standing, elbows rubbing, with her man. She walks over to Justin and reaches up to give him a kiss hello.

"You are so cold. Come here … let me warm you up." Justin wraps his arms around Nicole pulling her in close enough that she can smell the beer on his breath.

"Thank you babe, it is freezing out tonight."

"I wish you would have let me pick you up, at least around the corner from your house or something."

"I am perfectly capable of walking …"

"Your car broke or something?" Alicia chimes in.

"No." Nicole responds shortly not looking at Alicia.

"So you what …" Alicia is waiting for an explanation she can make fun of.

"Don't you have somewhere to be or someone to do or something?" Jill walks into the room attacking Alicia at sight.

"And you are who?" Alicia glares back at Jill.

"So, you made it …" Jill ignores Alicia and speaks directly to Nicole.

"Yeah it was a little touch and go for a bit but once the rents were asleep I headed over."

"So are you heading back before they get up or just heading to my house?"

"I have not decided yet," Nicole lets the yet hang in the air as she smiles up at her man leaving the space for his invitation to spend the night together instead. In her mind though she knows she will have to be home in bed before her parents come in to wake her in the morning. Alicia leaves the room and the fun begins. Everyone is moving from one room to the next while some start passing out or getting sick.

"I think your man is a little bit sick," Jillian warns Nicole.

"He will be okay, I have already started watering down his drinks."

"So how are you feeling?"

"A little buzzed but good," Nicole responds with glazed eyes.

"Check it out … our friends have had a bit too much

to drink," Jillian says pointing to Adria and Sarah. They are sitting on either side of the guy that will play Romeo in Nicole's drama club play. They are literally hanging off of either arm and glaring at each other in competition. The guy however is staring at Nicole with a slight smile on his face. Nicole looks back to Jillian quickly once she notices.

"Where is Cameron? I thought he would be here by now."

"He text me a bit ago that he has to work a little overtime and will be here as soon as he can, until then we have to go tease the girls." Jillian is pulling Nicole's arm as she leads her over to the three in the middle of the room.

"Hey girls," Jillian starts with a smile aimed at Adria and Sarah.

"Hey yourself," they say back with an inquisitive look towards Jillian.

"How about you two let the man stand," Jillian jokes at them winking towards Romeo. Romeo has kept his sights on Nicole the entire time and now offers his hand to her.

"We were not formally introduced yesterday, my name is Ryan and I will be playing Romeo," she takes his hand lightly and pulls away quickly.

"So what made you want to be in the play?"

"You are playing Juliet … I could think of nothing

better than being your Romeo," Ryan smiles warmly as he says this to her.

"Thank you I am flattered that you think I am that good," Nicole is unsure of what else to say thinking that Ryan is apparently a smooth talker.

"You are, and I was going to ask you if we could maybe do some practice together so that I can catch up?"

"Sure we will have plenty of time during drama club after school."

"I meant just me and you. Perhaps after the drama club lets out."

" I uh … well I would like to help you out but I am not sure that is such a good idea," Nicole is unsure as she answers but her friends can see that she really wants to tell him yes. Jillian is almost laughing at the awkward flirting going on between her friend and this new guy. Nicole looks around after every statement for Justin, unsure of how he will react if he sees her talking and standing so close with this other guy. Normally Justin would show up and introduce himself but with drinking and friends around to impress he may act a bit jealous and mean.

"What if I ask that boyfriend of yours? I know he won't mind as long I tell him up front that I need the help and that it is good practice for you. He would not want to be the one to hold you back from your dreams," Ryan is smiling because he knows that he is right, guilt goes a long way with Justin.

"We can get together and practice. I don't need his

permission but I will tell him about it." Nicole feels kind of silly once she hears Ryan explain it like that, as if Justin was another parent of hers instead of her boyfriend.

"I look forward to it and any other time I can spend with you," Ryan says, more blatantly flirting now.

"Really... Well I look forward to turning you into the best Romeo ever," Nicole replies.

Jillian has held her tongue as long as she can and interjects, "So should we start practicing now? How about the kissing scene?"

"Jillian!" Nicole states sharply giving her a look.

"Well it's that or the scene where you lay down together to die," Jillian responds shrugging.

"Yeah, that is the only parts we know," Adria says while waving her hand back and forth in front of herself and Sarah, her drink spilling along the way.

"I would be happy to start with any part the lady wishes," Ryan says jokingly and bows in front of her. This causes Nicole to laugh and bend forward bringing Ryan's face within inches of her own. They pause for a moment looking into each other's eyes. There is a tense moment and Nicole feels the electricity between them as his sight travels from her eyes to her lips and back. Nicole feels drawn to him and even leans forward a bit more before Sarah grabs her arm pulling her away.

"Hey that is my man. I saw him first and you can't have him. You already have a boyfriend. That's not fair,"

Sarah is drunk and does not mean to be accusing or cause trouble for her friend but does.

"Hey she is just having fun. Besides everyone needs to move on sometimes," Jillian is defending Nicole as well as taking this time to voice her opinion on Nicole's need to move on from Justin.

"Hey, nothing happened and ..." Nicole is cut off by Ryan.

"I do not belong to anyone and Nicole I hope you do move on, I should be upfront in saying that. And when you do move on I hope I have the opportunity to show you that I deserve a chance to treat you well."

"I am with Justin and my friend is just drunk," Nicole walks away.

Nicole walks down the hallway towards the front door but everyone is hanging out by the door so she heads towards the bedrooms instead. She does not realize it but Ryan has followed her. She stops and leans her back against the wall in a corner where she is alone. He appears shortly after and begins to apologize.

"I am sorry about that. I did not mean to cause trouble or embarrass you. I think that you are wonderful and that you go unappreciated. Someday maybe you will realize this and when you do I hope that I am there. That is all. I know I sound like some crazy kid with a crush but really it is more than that. Anyways. I am sorry and I hope I did not ruin your night," Ryan starts to turn away.

"No, don't go. You are nice and you did not ruin my

night. I have had a little more to drink than I realized I guess. I did feel something for a moment there, close to you and I am sure it was the alcohol. I hope to get to know you better but as friends or … I don't know. Do you really think that I am unappreciated?" The drinking was starting to take a toll on Nicole and she is having a little more trouble keeping her thoughts straight. Her phone starts to vibrate and she pulls it out while Ryan stands watching. It is a text message from Jillian saying, "screw Justin go for it".

"Your boyfriend I guess," Ryan says.

"No my friend. She thinks I have been with Justin too long and that I need to try something new. She apparently thinks that you are the something new."

"What do you think?" Ryan asks.

"That I am drunk and tired and that is why I want to kiss you."

"Really?"

"Yeah so I should find Justin and behave. I will see you at school," Nicole moves to go past him and in the seconds as there bodies rub against each other in passing she imagines staying there and him wrapping his arms around her. He is after all very toned and very cute. He has dark hair, tan skin, light blue eyes, and dimples that show every time he smiles. He seemed to know a lot more about Nicole than she ever knew about him. Once she is past Ryan in the hall she texts Jillian back asking her where Justin was. Jillian texts back to Nicole that she does not want to know. So Nicole starts to get agitated and text again. Jillian answers that Justin is in the kitchen. Nicole proceeds through everyone towards the kitchen but Jillian meets her in the hall just outside the dinning area.

"You should not go in there and if you do remember that everyone is drunk and you really should go hang out with Ryan… he is cool and cute."

Nicole cuts Jillian off, "Your rambling. What's up?" Jillian knows her friend has had too much to drink and knows it will affect her judgment but at the same time is kind of glad that her friend will see her boyfriend in true form. Justin is a good guy; Jillian just thinks that Nicole needs to date someone else for a change since the two of them seem to have been together forever and the relationship has become too much like an old married couple and no fun.

They both walk into the kitchen just as Justin is doing a body shot off of Alicia's chest. He finishes the shot and looks up seeing Nicole standing there he waves to her to join in the fun. Alicia looks over with an evil smirk on her face. Nicole thinks to herself, of all the people he could be playing around with it had to be her. Deep down Nicole knows that he would not be hanging with Alicia and acting this way if he was sober and not with the guys. But the alcohol was taking precedence over any kind of rational thought and she followed her gut instead. Nicole's anger, which would normally lead her to try to fight with Alicia, instead sent her looking for Ryan. He was right where she left him. She walks up close to him so that their bodies are only barely touching, brushing against each other slightly. She looks him in the eyes and asks him the deciding question.

"Did you mean everything you said?"

"Yes I did. You are..." He does not get the chance to finish his statement because she pushes her body against his bringing her lips to his. He is caught off guard but happily joins in the kiss. He seems unsure of where to put his hands, he wants to wrap them around her and pull her in but is afraid that if he does she will pull away. So for a moment they stand suspended but together. It only last for a moment though as he takes the chance and wraps himself around her pulling her close to him and continuing the very passionate kiss.

"What the ..." Justin enters the hallway looking for Nicole since she left and did not join in the fun with him.

The two kissing jump back away from each other startled that there is someone else around. Nicole looks at Justin and then at Ryan and she starts to cry. Ryan quickly feeling like the situation could be misinterpreted by the tears reacts to Justin, "Hey she just came in here and I don't know something must have upset her and I had told her..."

Justin interjects, "Shut up man. I am not talking to you."

"Hey you can't talk to him like that …you just go be with Alicia," Nicole says while grinding her teeth.

"What are you talking about?"

"You in there with her," Nicole answers.

"I think I should let you two talk," Ryan says as he slides past the arguing couple in the hall. They ignore him and continue on.

"Everyone was drinking and doing shots that was not just her and me," Justin is slurring his words a little bit.

"Well everyone is screwing her too does that mean you will too?" Nicole is angrier at Alicia than she really is at Justin.

"You know I would not. I love you. But you are over here all over that guy and stuff."

"He told me I was special and wonderful and that you did not appreciate me. I thought he was right and I was saying thank you."

"Is that how you always say thank you?"

"You know it isn't I was just mad at you for sucking on Alicia's tits."

"That is not what was happening your drunk lets just chill out together for a while."

"In other words you're tired of arguing?"

"How do you start a fight about a fight? I am going back with the guys I don't want to deal with this shit."

"Fine. I am going home."

"How?"

"What do you mean how? However I want. Bye,"

Nicole pushes past Justin, waves at Jillian and the girls and heads for the door.

"Hey, at least take the three musketeers with you."

"Like you give a shit," Nicole takes her jacket from the chair by the door and pushes her way out the front door. Once outside she stops on the front porch putting her coat on and taking a deep breath.

CHAPTER FIVE
The Way Home

—————— ◊ ——————

Outside the house the wind is blowing and the frost is setting in. It is really cold and the shock of the cold against Nicole's face instantly starts to sober her up. She takes a couple steps and hesitates, should she go back in and make up with Justin or maybe have the girls take her home? It would be better to walk and sober up probably before trying to go into the house with her parents sleeping. She starts walking. Throughout her walk home there are very few cars on the road, but every time one drives by Nicole stops walking to look. In her mind she pictures Justin pulling up to apologize. She imagines spending the rest of the night just the two of them. In a way she was even getting more mad at him that he had not shown up yet to make amends. Maybe Jillian was right and it was time to move on.

Nicole is about half way home when she hears the truck pull onto the street she is walking home on. She stops and turns to see who it is. It is an older truck and she does not recognize it, however she does like it. It reminds her of the car shows she sometimes attends with Justin. The truck is an old model but restored to look new. It is an old style truck with the big fenders and short truck bed. The body looks clean and the paint looks brand new. It looks and sounds nice but not too overdone. There is not any fire or any other cheesy designs painted onto it. She keeps walking as the truck passes but as it passes the guy driving looks over at her. She can not help but notice that he is cute. The truck slows to a stop a few hundred feet in front of her and the driver leans out the window waiting for her to catch up to the truck.

She is a little wary of the truck and this guy that she does not know but she is also drunk and this guy is cute. She likes the attention and the fact that she is so hurt by her boyfriend makes it easy to think of this guy as her knight in shining armor stopping to save her on this cold night. She continues to think of scenarios that include this guy being the guy of her dreams as she gets closer to the truck. She wonders if she is stumbling at all or if the driver can even tell she's drunk. The guy is smiling as she walks up next to where the truck is stopped.

"It is awfully late and cold for you to be out walking,"

the driver starts with his head still hanging out the window.

"Yeah, I am on my way home," Nicole responds.

"Well, it probably isn't good for you to be walking. Would you like a ride home?" The driver asks casting a smile that Nicole feels could light up the street.

"Well, I should be okay. I am almost home," Nicole wants to ride with this cute guy but is unsure if she should.

"It is up to you. I just hate to see a pretty girl out in the cold like this. Don't you have a boyfriend that could have given you a ride?"

"That is a long story. He is being a jerk, we got in a fight tonight," Nicole wonders to herself why she is telling this stranger so much.

"Well it is his loss. If you need a ride I am happy to oblige."

"Ok. It is not too far. My name is Nicole."

"My name is Seamus. Hop on in."

The driver, Seamus, pulls his head back into the truck and reaches across the passenger side to unlock the door for Nicole. Nicole steps around the front of the truck looking at the large grill and bright lights on the front. They seem to be smiling at her but that could just be the few too many drinks she had at the party. She reaches the door and hesitates for a moment thinking that she should not ride with a stranger. On the other hand, she thinks, it is freezing and he is nice and really cute, besides everyone is a stranger at first.

Seamus looks to be about early twenties or so with short hair and a thin mustache. He has a strong square jaw line and a large smile. Now that Nicole is in the car she can see that he is dressed in jeans and a t-shirt. He has a normal build and seems like he is pretty tall. She sets back into the seat and tells Seamus to continue going straight. She starts to ask him questions but he seems to answer them all with questions about her.

"Do you live around here?"

"Just came into the area. Have you always lived here?" Seamus asks in return.

"Yes, me and my parents. Where did you move from?" Nicole feels like he avoided her question.

"Close by. Are you an only child?" Seamus probes further into Nicole's life.

"Yes. How about you?"

"Yes, me too. What's your boyfriend like? You said you got into a fight?" Seamus is most interested in this part of the conversation.

"Yeah he made me jealous with another girl hanging on him and then I kissed this other guy and stuff. I expected him to come after me but I guess he does not care," Nicole again wonders to herself why she is sharing all of this with someone she does not know.

"I am sure he cares maybe he was hurt over the kiss," Seamus defends the boyfriend.

"I don't know. Turn at the next right," Nicole doesn't want to think that it could be her fault so she avoids the conversation and returns to giving directions.

"Ok." Seamus mumbles.

It is quiet for a moment as they come up to the right hand turn but as they reach the turn Seamus does not turn he continues straight. Nicole feels her stomach go into her throat a little but hopes that maybe she is just overreacting.

"I said to turn right. You missed it."

"Oh. Sorry I must not have heard you. I will turn around," he smiles at her as he says this.

"Ok. Thanks," Nicole smiles back feeling unsure.

The truck starts into a u-turn but as they reach the top of the turn Seamus lets his arm relax on the wheel and gives a quick reach with the other over to Nicole. He grabs her head and smashes it forward onto the dashboard of the truck. In a matter of seconds Nicole is unconscious and the truck is straightening back into the direction it was headed. Nicole's head is hanging forward as a thin line of blood trickles down her forehead. The driver, Seamus, smiles. He straightens up and continues driving on in the direction he wanted to go. It is not far to his destination now that he has Nicole with him and he is excited to get there.

CHAPTER SIX
The Investigation

———————— ◊ ————————

I t was late in the afternoon and everyone was both tired and hungry. Special Agent Fisher was pushing his team to come up with something new. They felt like they were running down the same leads over and over and getting nowhere. The more information they found the further away they got from understanding the serial killer. They have been reviewing the same information for almost 72 hours. They needed a break, Fisher tells them to go home and change into some clean cloths, eat, and return in a couple hours. They all headed out to return in a few hours. While they are out Fisher continues to review the files in front of him. He is searching for something they all missed.

They have pulled and went through each of the victim's

information, credit cards, phone bills, bank accounts, you name it and they looked at it. They found no connection between the victims. The similarities stopped at young, attractive high school students. They are all female with the same approximate height and weight but different hair and eye color. They had nothing tying them together to help the team get an idea of how he chose them. This made the team think that he was not picking his victims based on someone he was trying to replicate, like an abusive mother or ex-girlfriend. Fisher felt like they may have run into a brick wall but then the phone rang.

"Fisher," he grabs the phone and has it up to his ear before the second ring.

"I have some new information for you. There was a high level of salt and caffeine in the liver of the last victim. I will check the other victim's for the same. This means that the killer administered something to the victim within approx. 5 hours of her death that contained high levels of both," the medical examiner informs Fisher.

"So then we know for sure that the killer did not just leave her somewhere to die. Do we have an idea of what he may have given to her?"

"No. I just know that at about 5 hours or so the body would have distributed the caffeine and it would have been far less traceable than it was. It must have been a large dose of caffeine. I would say more than a traditional cup of coffee or soda."

"So what do you think it was?" Fish wants more of an answer.

"Personally, I think that it was not given to her in a regular type of food. I think the killer may have added caffeine to something he gave her to speed up her metabolism and make her starve faster. I could be wrong though. I can only say for sure what the body tells me and that is that there is a high concentrate of caffeine."

"Thank you. Let me know if you find anything else."

There is still a little time before the rest of the team will return so Agent Fisher decides to return home to shower and change. He would return and share the news with his team so that they could discuss what this meant for this killer they were trying so hard to understand.

When Fisher returns the rest of the team is already there discussing the next best thing to try. Fisher walks in and sits down listening to them until there is a break in conversation and then stands to give them what he learned earlier from the medical examiner. Agent Carr seems the most interested and responds before anyone else has a chance.

"So the killer stays with them while they die, so that would make me believe it is not about abandonment. If he is increasing the caffeine to make the death quicker then he is showing some empathy for the victim," Carr starts as she waves her arms in the air and lands with one hand cupping her chin.

"Or he needs them to die faster so that he can start the process over again. Maybe it is something in the beginning of the killing that excites him and he needs the victim to die fast so that he can again get that excitement from a new victim," Burke offers.

"That may be but then why kill them at all, why not leave them there and not help them die faster? He could keep himself concealed and enjoy the kidnapping part and then not finish it," Vickers wants to point out that this idea of an element of compassion in a killer makes no sense.

"I think it is more than that. I think maybe he wants to see them die and does not want to wait for it. He pushes it along for the excitement of it," Fisher states.

"If he wants the death to come faster then why not just physically kill them himself, strangle them or something. He takes no other action than to push the body to naturally die," Dalton seems frustrated with the killer.

"Well maybe that is his trigger the torture of a slow death. Maybe he was starved as a child by his young mother and feels he needs to get back at her. The victim's are just his way of acting out what he imagined doing to his mother throughout his childhood. He probably did it the first time not knowing how much enjoyment he would get from it and then continued when he found it was the only thing that could excite him. The first time could very well be once he got old enough to starve the person that starved him. Fish, we should start cross referencing old cases of death in young women from starvation," Carr offers.

"Unless the excitement is derived from the hypothermia and not the starvation. We are forgetting to factor that into these deaths. What if they died from the cold and not the lack of food? The examiner does not seem to be sure which one came first," Vickers asks.

"It may be symbolic, the cold I mean. When you feel alone and hurt, in this case starving, you may feel cold and distant from the world. He may be acting metaphorically by leaving them in the cold to die," Burke offers.

"Ok, so what do we think we are looking for?" Fisher addresses the whole group knowing that Carr will be the one to answer.

"A male, probably mid twenty's to early thirty's based on the young age of the girls. They are not too young suggesting pedophilia but not old enough for him to consider them equal. He is probably a loner feeling abandoned by the world would make him want to leave the victim calling for help. Probably has a history of mental illness, most likely depression. That would be why he would want the victim feeling desperate. He is moving over a large area so either he has no strong family ties or he is trying to run from the family he has. He leaves no fingerprints, DNA, or anything else of himself behind not even the rope he uses to bind them, so he is detailed and careful, not careless. He would also be a little detached since he lets them die on their own he probably likes to watch and not interact with the victim. There have been no bruises to suggest him grabbing or beating the victim so they probably go with him on their own accord, giving the appearance that he must seem like a normal guy. He also may have a phobia or issue with touch since he seems to not touch the victims," Carr lays out an outline of what she believes the killer is like.

"Or maybe that is his trigger. Maybe he is trying to have normal relationships with these girls and once they touch him he loses control and binds them believing that they are out to hurt him, maybe he was abused," Vickers interjects.

"Well, outside of the why let us focus on getting a description to the local police departments and let us start running down deaths in the surrounding areas that are similar to these murders." Fisher wants to move forward with the investigation and feels they are starting to put together a good enough idea of characteristics of this killer to find him.

"Well, at least we now know that he does not leave, so if we monitor missing persons perhaps we can track the people that go missing in the surrounding areas that match the appearance of the previous victims. See if we can find any previous killings that show a pattern or escalation," Carr offers looking to Burke for some help with this idea.

"Kid, you know what to do. Get into that computer

of yours and find us something." Fisher directs the order to Burke.

"I'll help him funnel it out and run down any leads. Dalton can help us follow on any leads we get from it," Vickers offers to Burke looking to Fisher for approval. Fisher nods his head in agreement.

"Fish, I will get the description out and talk with all the local law enforcement, in the meantime," Dalton states.

"Check the maps and see what roads are most easily reached from the locations of bodies. See if there is a pattern of movement that we can track, like if he seems to be jumping on and off interstates or using a lot of side streets. I want to know how familiar he is with the areas he is hunting in," Fisher directs to Dalton.

"I'm on it." Dalton states as he leaves the group.

"You and me," Fisher points at Carr. "We will talk to the friends again of the last few victims and see if anyone knew of a new boyfriend, friend, co-worker. Let's see how this guy fit into the victim's lives. They must have either trusted him or were caught so off-guard that they did not have time to react. Maybe they saw someone talking to them on another occasion that they did not know or something. Let's see what we can find."

"Alright. Let's go. We can start with the most recent victim first," Carr headed out the door just behind Fisher, both of them pulling on their coats.

CHAPTER SEVEN
Sunday

———— ◊ ————

Nicole wakes up to water splashing hard in her face. It stings and she is confused. Her vision is fuzzy and her body aches. The water stops shortly after her waking but she still can't seem to get a grip on her surroundings. She is soaking wet, she can feel it in her bones and she is on the floor. A hard floor, no carpet or flooring just plywood. She shutters from the cold and can not tell where she is. She hears footsteps but can not make out where they are coming from. She tries to move and can not seem to do anything but wiggle on the ground. Her hands and feet are stuck together and the more she tries to pull them apart the more they begin to hurt. Her arms are behind her and she looks down to focus on a rope that wraps around her stomach and seems to be holding her hands down tied to her back. She continues to focus and look around her.

"Hello…" she shouts into the open air around her. There is no answer. She remembers hearing footsteps a few moments before but can not tell if they were just in her mind or if they were real. She is not sure what to do with herself so she just tries to look around as much as she can to take in any clues that are offered to her. It looks to her as if she is in a house that is not built yet. There is a stairway next to her that is under construction and the windows that are up are covered with plastic. There is dirt everywhere and paint spots on floor around her. She seemed to be on the second floor since the floor was not cement. She could see some tools left behind by the workers. This gives her hope that they will return soon and find her.

"Anyone there? Hey … Is anyone there?" Every time that she shouts there is an echo and then dead silence. For a moment she thinks she hears a car out on the road but is not sure how far or close it may be. She starts to remember the ride home and the guy that picked her up. She can not remember how she got here though and feels lost in her own thoughts. Her parents must be looking for her by now, she feels reassured that everything will be okay by that thought. She lays in silence for a while trying to listen to every noise around her. Every time that she moves she hears the floor creak underneath her. She waits to see what will happen to her.

Her kidnapper, Seamus is close by at a local convenience store looking for some specific supplies. He keeps his head low but is courteous to everyone he passes. He is completely calm and feels better than he has in days. He buys himself some food, easy items like cup-o-noodles, peanut butter, jelly, and bread. He buys caffeine tablets and water bottles, even a new knife. He starts to leave and almost forgets to pick up the large container of salt that is essential to him. He walks back down that isle and runs into a group of kids.

"Excuse me," he offers as he bumps the shoulder of one of the boys.

"Sure, man." The boy responds not even looking up from the magazine he is holding.

Seamus reaches the bags but has to say again to the group, "excuse me."

The girls move out of the way looking up at him, "No problem."

The first girl looks to her friend at her side and smiles. Once Seamus has left the isle she whispers to her friend, "Hey Jill, that guy was cute."

"Don't you ever think about anything else?" Jill looks over at Adria, smiling also.

"Yeah, but he was," Adria laughs.

"All of you are just too boy crazy," Justin says as he looks up from his magazine for the first time.

"Hey have you talked to Nicole yet?" Jill asks.

"No, I figure she is still mad at me."

"Well, she has not called me either. So she either got busted or is mad at all of us for not helping her out last night and giving her a ride home," Jill is directing this statement at Justin who is ignoring her.

"Well there was a lot going on last night. Maybe she needs time to think, to reevaluate her feelings," Sarah pushed.

"Hey, last night was nothing. Everything is fine," Justin stated getting a little annoyed.

"Didn't seem like nothing to me." A voice stated from the next isle.

"What?" Justin responded trying to see who was inviting themselves into the conversation.

"It did not seem like nothing to me," Ryan stated shortly as he continued down the isle beside the group.

"What the hell do you know," Justin was moving his way towards Ryan and the girls could tell there was a fight coming on.

At the same time Cameron walks into the store to hurry the group along and sees that Justin is heading into some trouble. It is easy to tell that Justin wants to fight with his quick pace and puffed up chest. Cameron looks over to see Ryan and quickly steps in between the two. He grabs Justin's arm and directs him outside.

"Why you got to get in the middle man. That guy has it coming," Justin complains to Cameron not really expecting an answer.

"Hey you don't need any trouble and Nicole was just

using that guy like you used what's her name. Give the guy a break. You know that you and Nicole will make up and that guy will be left dreaming about her. Cut him some slack."

"Yeah I guess your right. How did you get so smart … oh yeah wisdom comes with old age," Justin smiled and playfully pushed Cameron back from him. Justin liked to tease Cameron that he was getting old. Secretly Cameron wished he could break away from this group and move on with people his own age. He loved Jillian though and was not ready to leave her quite yet and with her comes the whole group. Moments later the group was packed into the car and heading to the movies, snacks in hand.

Meanwhile, Nicole is still listening to the sounds outside as she lays frustrated on the floor. She thinks she can hear many different noises but as time goes on she realizes that just about every noise is caused by her imagination. Silence is awful she realizes. She starts shouting out for help and trying to move across the floor. She moves and moves but seems to get nowhere. She seems to be flopping around like a fish out of water and she feels helpless and starts to cry. Through her sobs she hears a car.

Seamus pulls passed the house under construction a few times before circling around the side street and walking through the back up to the house where he has put Nicole. He walks calmly along, a smile on his face.

He feels like skipping, he is glad that he found Nicole when he did, he was tired of looking. He walks up to the house quietly so he does not make any noise and alert her to his arrival. He likes to listen to them trying to get away and call for help. He does not hear much other than her crying. He is happy at that. He hates when they scream a lot, it gives him a headache. He enters the house and walks up the stairs knowing that she must have heard the creak of the stairs and knows he is there now.

"Hello… Who's there? Help me please…" Nicole shouts towards the stairs. She can hear someone coming up but is not sure if that is good or bad. Her stomach has butterflies as she waits to see who will appear.

"Hello again," Seamus announces at the top of the stairs as he smiles over to her.

"Hello again? Are you fucking kidding me?" Nicole's frustration is brought to the surface.

"Yes, hello again," he is playing with her.

"Who the hell are you and what are you doing to me. Let me go!"

"That is not going to happen. I told you … I'm Seamus."

His smile is giving Nicole the creeps. What is this guys problem and what is he going to do to her? She is racking her brain for escape plans and ways to get this guy to untie her. She is coming up blank all she can think about is how she is going to fight. She is not going to let this guy win. She wants to tear his eyes out and run away.

"How are you feeling?" He asks her with a look of concern on his face.

"How am I feeling? Like I want to kill you," Nicole can not believe this guy.

"I understand that feeling but that won't happen. Are you hungry?"

"No. I don't want anything from you."

"Alright."

Seamus sits down across the room from Nicole and stares at her. Nicole can not figure out what this guy wants and she is worried that once it becomes night he may do something to her. She has to think of a way out of here. He just sits still, staring at her like he is waiting for something. She thinks maybe it is sex that he is after and if she acts interested or trusting that maybe he will untie her and she can get away.

"Seamus. You know you don't have to tie me up to get me to spend time with you. I wanted to be with you that is why I took a ride from you," Nicole offered trying to muster up a smile that looked more like she just ate something she did not like.

"Is that how you always are? Run out on your boyfriend with the first guy that drives by?"

"No. Your different," Nicole lets that hang in the air unable to think of anything else.

"Yes, I am. I am going to show you."

This last statement scared Nicole, she was not sure what he meant and she knew that him being different was not in any way meant to be a "good" kind of different. What is he going to show her? She is too afraid to ask. She frantically attempts to get her hands out of the rope they were tied in. The more that she tries the more her wrist and hands sting and ache. She could tell they were bruised and bleeding based on how they began to slide against the rope like they were wet. The more she tugs on her hands the more she realizes that she is also cutting into her own stomach. Since the rope is wrapped around her waist then tied to her hands behind her back the more she moves her hands the more it moves the rope back and forth around her waist. The pain in her wrist is one thing but the pain in her stomach is unbearable so she stops moving turning her attention back to the lunatic in front of her.

"So tell me why is it that bitches like you feel like they are better than everyone else?" Seamus has a genuine look of intrigue on his face as he asks this question.

"I am not better than anyone else," Nicole is confused by this question.

"You think you are too good for your boyfriend and that any guy would want you. I am sure you use that to control all the boys."

"No, I love my boyfriend we were just fighting last night. He will be looking for me you know. So will my parents."

"They have to realize that you are gone first and then check with all your friends… by the time they even start looking you will be halfway gone. Besides they won't find you here."

"Your wrong they will come looking and they will find me and you will go away forever," She snarls through the tears now streaming down her face.

"We will see won't we?"

"What can I do to make you let me go?" Nicole asks, hoping again for some insight that will tell her how to get away.

"Nothing," Seamus stated with a sad look as if he really felt sorry for her.

"Nothing?" Nicole questioned back.

"You are only good to me here. You will stay with me till the end."

"What end? End of what?"

"Till the end." With that Seamus leaned back and began eating a sandwich while silence filled the air. Nicole closed her eyes, knowing that watching him eat would make her more hungry and hoping deep down that somehow if she closed her eyes tight enough that when she opened them again he would be gone. It is torture to watch someone else eat when you are so hungry. She kept her eyes closed for a long time and when she did finally open them Seamus was no longer in front of her and she began to cry again.

CHAPTER EIGHT
Monday

———— ◊ ————

Nicole's parents spent all day Sunday worrying about her and contacting her friends by Monday morning it seemed that something had happened to Nicole. Her father just did not believe that Nicole ran away just because of the argument over her college. Jillian had come by in the evening and it was official that she was not staying at any of her friend's houses. As everyone returned to school on Monday the news that Nicole was missing spread fast and by the end of the day the students were all at Nicole's house waiting for the police.

The police arrived and Nicole's mother explained the argument that she had with Nicole and that when she went to get Nicole out of bed on Sunday she was gone. For the first time Jillian and Justin both began to tell the truth at the same time. This caused some confusion and the officers asked them to speak one at a time. Jillian starts.

"She snuck out on Saturday night to go to a party with all of us," Jillian says waving her arm around the room at everyone. Instantly the officer's face begins to change and frustration fills his tone.

"We got in a fight and she left in the middle of the night to walk home," Justin adds.

"Where was this party?

"A friend's house… it's about a half hour walk from here."

"What kind of drugs was she doing?"

"Huh? None. She may have had a couple drinks but no drugs," Adria reacts at first with amazement at the question and then looks towards the ground with shame as she realizes Nicole's parents are watching her.

"So she started walking home and no one gave her a ride?"

"No," the friends all say in unison and look towards the ground.

"You let her walk all that way in the middle of the night?" Nicole's father says to Justin with an angry look on his face.

"I'm sorry, I thought she was fine she walked there and she was mad at me and … I'm sorry," Justin stutters his eyes shifting down and to the side avoiding eye contact with Nicole's dad.

"No one has heard from her since then?"

"No. She usually send me a text when she gets home but she was upset about Justin so I just figured she forgot and then when her parents called me I got worried and came over and helped them call everywhere. She has not answered her phone at all…it goes straight to voicemail," Jillian explains.

"Well, with all the information and description you gave me if you just have a picture I can take with me I will be on my way."

"On your way to find my daughter," Nicole's mom pushes.

"Yes, mam. I will get the word out right away and let you know if we find out anything at all."

"Thank you."

The officer leaves and the room is quiet. No one really knows what to think. Sarah continues to cry off and on and Justin looks like he is carrying a ten-ton weight on his back. They all continue to sit quietly while all of them feel guilty inside thinking that they each in some own way could have prevented it.

Meanwhile, the FBI is receiving the call from the police department that they have a missing persons matching the description they have put out to all the departments. Fisher receives the call and decides it is the best lead they have so he has the team pack up and head out to the police department to assist in finding the girl and hopefully the killer he is looking for. On the way there they all review the missing person case as well as try to tie it to the killer they are looking for. This becomes an easy task very fast.

"So, the missing girl was walking home alone in the middle of the night and no one has seen her since. She is 17 years old and attends the local high school. Attractive girl and popular. It was also reported that she may have been drinking, that may have impaired her ability to fight back and made her an easier target," Fisher is describing Nicole's case to his team.

"So we are starting two days behind the killer if he took her Saturday night. How long are we thinking we have from when he takes her until she dies?" Burke asks looking towards Carr.

"Well, the average time it takes for a person to either starve to death or die from hypothermia both are anywhere from a few days to over week or so. It is hard to say, some people can survive remarkable things and others may only last a night. Luckily the weather is not continually below freezing and she will not be malnourished to start."

"Don't forget that this killer is trying to speed it along also," Dalton interjects.

"That is true. If it would typically take a week I would say five days with the extra caffeine and salt. There is just no way of truly knowing since the other cases the bodies were not found for some time after death, even weeks with the last victim," Carr is beginning to doubt herself as all the different scenarios play out in her mind.

"There are a lot of things that come into consideration let's just focus on finding her as soon as possible. If we find her still alive we find him," Fisher tries to refocus the group on what they know.

"So, he did not travel far before finding a new victim and he picked her up on an unplanned walk home from a party. Do we think he is watching his victims or just striking at any opportunity?" Burke asks.

"We can not be sure but I think it is about the opportunity," Carr jumps in with her thoughts.

"Kid, what do you have for us?" Fisher directs to Burke.

"I have been running list of people that have either died from starvation or hypothermia. I am looking at a target range of over the last three years and then breaking it down to females and then trying to sort by age group. The problem is that there are so many to sort through it is taking some time," Burke answers.

"There are a lot of cases popping up that were determined to be homeless or prostitutes and not what we are looking for," Vickers offers to help explain Burke's findings.

"Why don't we lessen the radius of the search and include a little higher age group to see if we can track if the killer started on someone close to him. Also look into criminal backgrounds and see if we have any situations where some of them were single and had a son," Dalton has not said much until now.

"Would you like to do it? Burke's running everything he can all at once, he will let you know as soon as he has something," Vickers becomes agitated with Dalton.

"Hey just trying to help the kid."

"Well, he doesn't need …"

"Hey I have something interesting here," Burke interrupts the arguing. "There was a woman killed in the same fashion within 25 miles of our first victim. She was not a mother but all the details of the case fit our killer. It wasn't noticed before because the victim was 38 years old and left in her own apartment. However, the medical examiner found high traces of caffeine and she was bound with rope similar to our recent victims."

"So he must have had some tie to her to want to kill her, especially if it was his first and he escalated from there. Find out everything you can about this case," Fisher orders Vickers and Burke.

"Already reviewing the case file."

"So, we may have a starting point. Since that victim the others were all found in abandoned areas or areas of new development where no one would frequent. See if you can search the area we are heading to for areas like that. Maybe we can have a list of places to search when we arrive at the station."

The FBI team is almost to the station but already Nicole feels weak and no one is even looking for her yet. She feels like the room is spinning. Her mouth is dry and she feels like there is something stuck on her tongue.

The pain that had started in her stomach a while after the growling stopped has now moved into her sides as if it were trying to crawl under her ribs and into her heart. She has not had a thing to eat or drink since Saturday night and now it is Monday night. She has never been this long without something to eat. She has had to watch her captor eat in front of her making sounds of satisfaction and getting practically giddy every time her stomach growled or she winced in pain. He was just finishing a grilled tuna sandwich as he began to talk to her again.

"You know they are talking about you on the radio, I am sure the TV also. They say what a wonderful young person you are and how much everyone is concerned about your safe return," he rolls his eyes before he continues. "We know the truth though, don't we? We know how you really are and what you will really do to people. How you will torture you boyfriend and the other boys in your life. I have to teach you a lesson before you can do that to them…"

"Do what to who? I won't hurt anyone I swear."

"That is what you want me to believe but I am not as naive as your little boyfriends. That is why your seduction will not work on me."

"I am not trying to do anything to you I just want to go home…" She was crying again but silently as the tears stream down her cheeks. She seems to be running out of tears. She swallows hard and asks him if she can have something to eat.

"Absolutely not, if I let you eat then I will not be able to. I can give you a drink."

Although the first part made no sense to her to have a drink would be heaven to her at this point so she nods in agreement. He walks over and begins to pour a water bottle over her mouth, at first she laps at the water like a dog, thirsty after a long run. It is only a minute of his laughing before she realizes that the water is filled with salt, she is more thirsty than before. She spits some out but the damage is done. She is so weak that she can not even muster up the words to fight with him. She instead lays her head to the ground and closes her eyes hoping to sleep and dream of being anywhere but where she is. It is not long before she sleeps but it seems like only seconds of sleep pass before she is awake again shivering and screaming.

The evening has settled into the middle of the night and there he stood over her pouring the container of salt all over her body and then spraying iced water onto her face and body. He knows the salt will increase the cold of the water and quicken the time it will take for her to freeze. Nicole's whole body stung but not only because of the water itself but because of the sting that has already crept through her body and numbed her hands and feet. The water beats on them causing a sharp pain to run up her arms and legs. She tries to maneuver into a protected fetal position but lacks the energy to maintain it. The rope has become tighter and keeps her from protecting herself also. She yells and moans in pain and he laughs. Once he stops he sits down to watch her squirm on the floor in the water. He looks at her as though he is trying to figure out what she is and she yells at him.

"What's wrong with you?"

"I have a very important job. I have to teach you," This is all he says before walking away and out of the house. She hears him leave and feels her body shivering and empty so she calls for help for a moment before subsiding to the fatigue that takes her back to sleep.

Seamus drives to the motel that he is staying at to take a warm shower. He feels like he can enjoy the shower now that she is all wet in the cold. He will shower, nap and return to her in the morning so that he may eat his breakfast. He gives a small smile to the desk clerk at the motel and a wave as he drives by to his room. He walks into the room turns on the TV and heads into the shower. He plays the news in the background because he knows that they will talk about his missing girl and wants to hear it so that he can enjoy himself. He listens as the warm water warms his body. Once he is done he sleeps for only a short bit before waking to the need that calls from inside him. He has to see the girl and know that she is suffering, it is the only thing that allows him to feel normal. He heads back out to the car as the sun begins to come up. It is Tuesday morning.

CHAPTER NINE
Tuesday

———— ◊ ————

"Fish," Dalton is frustrated with the local police department and is having some trouble hiding it. "They say they don't have the manpower to search all the locations that we gave them and are waiting for us to tell them where she is."

"Calm down. Gather them together so that we can explain to them what we are looking for and see if we can convince them that we are on the same side and need their help."

"I will see if I can give them a profile to work with as well as stress the importance of time," Carr offers trying to help the situation.

"Excuse me," an officer walked into the room, "a friend of the missing girl wants to speak with one of you."

"Just a moment," Fisher responds and nods at Carr to handle it.

Carr walked out in between the desk laid out in the department to the waiting area where the girl stood. She noticed that the girl was wringing her hands together in nervousness. She wondered what secret this girl could have possibly thought was important enough to come down to the station by herself and ask for a FBI agent. She walked up slowly offering her hand and introducing herself. Jillian took her hand and responded, "I am Nicole's best friend, Jill. I am not sure that it means anything but on the TV they made her dad say that even the smallest thing made a difference and for everyone to call in tips and such. I wanted to tell you something."

Carr waves towards the seat that Jillian has stood from and takes a seat next to her looking into her face with her own concerned look. She asks Jillian to continue on with what she has to tell her.

"The night Nicole left the party there was this other guy from school that really liked her. They kissed and Justin caught them that was part of the fight that all started with Alicia."

"Who is Justin and who is Alicia?" Carr asks.

"Justin is her boyfriend and Alicia is a girl that likes him. But the other guy his name is Ryan and he is in a play with Nicole. Romeo and Juliet. He may have something to do with it but I am not sure but I wanted to tell you in case it was important but I did not want to say it in front of her parents or Justin, you know?" Jillian is rambling on.

With a soft look on her face Carr responds, "Thank you that may help us and I appreciate you caring enough to let us know. I am going to have you give an officer the information for this Ryan guy and we will follow up on it."

"Ok," Carr leads her to the officer and heads to the back of the office. She could not tell Jillian that they already suspected a serial killer had Nicole. That information needed to remain confidential for the time being. She returned to the conference room and shook her head to say it was nothing to Fisher who was already discussing the circumstance of finding both the killer and the missing girl with the officers. Dalton stands in the corner with his arms crossed over his chest and Burke is continuously working on his laptop with Vickers looking over his shoulder and up at Fisher every so often. Carr strides into the center of the room picking up where Fisher stops.

"The location is more than important in a case like this because this killer has picked a very specific type of place for specific reasons. He is someone that is not from this area so he should stand out some and he will use the location he has chosen for the duration of his time with the victim. Our best bet at this point in time is to find him. We are working against the clock. She has already been out there in the below freezing temperatures and from what we know about this killer she has also been starving for a full three days already we need to start searching. We need your help to search so that we can continue to figure out who this guy is. What we know so far is …" Carr is interrupted by one of the younger officers.

"No offense but it sounds like you don't know anything so far."

"Thank you for interrupting to share your opinion but what I was about to tell you was what we know so far about this particular killer. He is probably mid twenty's to early thirty's based on the young age of the girls. He is probably a loner feeling abandoned would make him want to leave the victim calling for help. He probably has a history of mental illness most likely depression. The killings may have started after a psychotic break. He may suffer from a borderline personality disorder. He is moving over a large area. He leaves no fingerprints, DNA, or anything else of himself behind not even the rope he uses to bind them, he is detailed and careful. There has been no evidence of him beating the victim so they probably go with him on their own accord, giving the appearance that he must seem like a normal guy. He removes the restraints once they are either too weak or already dead leaving us with little evidence. We need you to continue looking for this missing girl and we will continue to look for the killer. Hopefully we will meet at the end before the girl dies or he moves on to a new victim."

"We all want to catch the guy and save the girl. He is probably driving a big vehicle, a van or truck, something easy to move them in without being noticed. He will need supplies so he will probably frequent a store nearby. We need to keep our minds open to leads without creating a panic in your city. We do not want the press or anyone else outside of this room to know we are chasing a serial killer. An obvious panic of people or the announcement that we are looking for a serial killer could do one of two things. He may run and kill again before we learn enough to catch him or he may enjoy the publicity and kill her faster and then kill more frequently. We do not want that at this point we may have some time so let's all use that time together. Thank you," Fisher ends with a thank you that is meant to say that they are all excused.

Meanwhile, Nicole is groggy but knows she is awake, parts of her body are numb yet inside she still seems to shiver. She is past feeling hungry and only feels empty. She slips back and forth in consciousness and has to figure out if she is awake or dreaming. This time she opens her eyes and sees beautiful butterflies circling around her, she imagines they want to help her. She wishes she could reach out to them since they are the only nice thing in her mind. Before long, they fly away and she realizes that Seamus is talking to her. She can not understand all of what he is saying, like a cell phone with bad reception her mind seems to keep cutting in and out.

"You are looking a little puffy…that is good. I assume you are still thirsty so I gave you some water but you did not seem to be there."

She did not understand what he meant or what he was saying. She stayed silent knowing that she felt too tired to form any words of her own. He continued to talk to her with a large smile on his face, she hates his face.

"You are learning what it is like … and that it is not nice. I was afraid you know when you got in my car that you would be a nice girl but once you told me about the boyfriend I knew you were not. You know that you are not a nice girl. So I get to teach you and protect them from you. You would have left them feeling empty and cold inside. Now you know how it feels. I am teaching you what it is like to feel dead before you are dead and know that it will not get better. You do know that don't you … for you it will never get better. You do help me though. I felt that way you know, how you are feeling now and then I discovered that I can feel better, as long as I am helping protect someone else from feeling this way, as long as I am teaching girls like you that you can't make us feel like this."

Nicole is hearing enough to put some pieces together but does not understand the degree to which his craziness goes. She knows he has been saying from the beginning that he was teaching her a lesson but she does not know from or for what. Now he says that she makes him feel better. He seems to be confused and sick. She senses that he is getting comfortable with her and knows this would be the time to try to get away but she can barely muster the energy to talk to him.

"I learned my lesson … can't you let me go now?"

"No, you lie. You only act like you learned your lesson to trick me I almost fell for that once. Besides I need you. I need you to starve so I can eat. I need you to freeze so I can be warm. I need you to die so that I can live," he smiles as he says this to her knowing that with the water and cold that she only has another couple days. He will have to start looking into where to go next so he leaves to go to the store and get some new maps and some more snacks. He wants to eat as much as he can before she dies because he knows he will not be able to eat once she is gone and he is looking for the next one to teach.

CHAPTER TEN
Wednesday

————— ◊ —————

There are dogs and cats playing together and Nicole thinks to herself, this just can't be right. It reminds her of the paintings where the dogs sit around a card table playing poker. That is impossible though and if she was not seeing it with her own eyes she would not believe it herself. Maybe he gave her something to make her see things. Where is he anyway and why can't I move my fingers or toes, she asks herself. She feels stronger for some reason and tries to raise her body up off the floor. She believes she is doing it and smiles, because she will beat this guy.

In reality she is not doing anything more than moving her head and this makes Seamus smile, he has seen it before. He knows that she must be hallucinating by now and he stands over her pouring onto her the water filled with salt and caffeine. She is lapping it up and swallowing as she smiles. When he speaks to her she does not change her focus or attention, she can no longer hear him. He lays down next to her hoping his body heat may warm her just enough to make it take a little longer for her to die. He is thankful for her he knows his ability to feel alive this last four days is because of her. He is also proud because he knows that she cannot hurt anyone anymore, he saved people from her. Girls like this should not be allowed to live. He wants to share this great feeling with everyone but knows that he must continue alone in secrecy, like superman, hiding his identity. He wants it to take longer for her to die. It is approaching the fifth day and he knows they all die by the seventh day. He makes sure of it. If more than a week goes by then they may find her or worse … others like her will go unpunished for the evil they do to the men around them.

Nicole whimpers and he leans in to her. He feels a little bit of happiness and a little bit of hate he will be glad when she is gone. Tomorrow he will remove the rope and clean the area free from any trace of him. By Friday it should be done and she will be gone.

Elsewhere, Agent Fisher is getting angry at the lack of assistance he is receiving from the police department. He knows that time is slipping by too fast for him to believe that they will find the missing girl alive. He calls a meeting with his team for a status report and to come up with ideas to light a fire under the police department. Everyone takes a seat and Agent Dalton speaks first.

"I can't believe this place. These idiots would rather let this girl die then work with anyone else. They think that by sticking together and ignoring any information we give them they can find her and say no thanks to us. What I would like to do with them and their ego …"

"Now, Dalton they just are not used to …" Agent Vickers tries to help.

"Oh, let it be …he is right let's get down to it. I don't want to waste minutes we need to find this victim griping about the lack of assistance or competence that we find here," Fish steps in.

"Well, Burke has been able to narrow down a few search areas. Let's see what he has," Agent Carr offers motioning to Burke.

Agent Burke motions to the laptop in front of him and they all lean in. "This city has extensive new development areas both in town and on the outskirts of town. The residential development is cast in blue while the commercial development areas are red. I have found at least three more victims that we had not previously known about that match the methods and signature of our killer. They were found in both residential and commercial buildings however, they all seem to be on the border of town. The highlighted areas would be the best spots I believe to look based on his travel patterns and previous discoveries."

"Why did you not just say those highlighted areas then kid?" Dalton growls.

"Because we will need to know how to explain it to the officers outside this room and because it is a lot of area to cover and we will need the manpower that the police department here can provide," Vickers steps in answering for Burke.

"Well it is a few square miles in each zone it will take quite a while and lots of bodies to search," Carr adds.

"So get the sergeant in here and we will get started," Fisher responds.

In a few moments there was a small crowd in the room and Agent Fisher was assigning teams to different areas on the map to start searching. He also announced that Agent Carr would be doing a press conference announcing the search and asking for anyone who wants to help with the search to meet at the police station. He explains that the team is hoping one of two things will happen; either the killer will involve himself in the search as expected based on his presumed borderline personality or that it will at least get enough people out on the streets to maybe find the girl in time. They need to move fast in an attempt to prevent creating a panic in the killer that makes him change his methods and kill her prematurely.

Not far from the police station, Jillian and Cameron are spending the evening with Justin, and the girls. They are keeping each other company during this confusing time. They are sitting in a pizza parlor when the news conference comes on the T.V. and they all fall silent as they watch.

"I am calling Nicole's parents, we should all be there searching," Jill states as soon as Agent Carr has stopped speaking.

" Yeah, let's go I want to find out where we are searching and when we can start," Justin is already out of his chair.

"Ok, we can all meet at the police station, like the news said," Cameron pulls Jillian up by her arm and nods to the other girls that it is time to go. They all leave together with a little more hope of finding their friend than they had before.

Seamus is taking his shower at the motel while the news plays in the background. He hears the plea for search parties and tries to listen closely. He does not hear if they know where to search or not but he decides that he must go back tonight and speed up the process.

CHAPTER ELEVEN
Wednesday Night and the Search

———————— ◊ ————————

Nicole is sleeping when Seamus returns but she is whimpering and whining in her sleep so he knows that she is in pain, she is suffering. That is all he could ever ask for, the only problem is that she can't live through this because she may help those that would want to stop him from performing his important work. He will have to join the search party so he can see where they are searching. He needs to keep them away long enough for her to pass. He does not want to do it himself because that would defeat the purpose of the punishment. He is a little angry that they are searching so soon because he will not be able to watch her tomorrow. The end is his favorite part, they way that they cry and the way that they look. She is no longer so pretty and she will be in pain and too weak to fight back although he will remove the ropes. He decides to eat before cleaning the area and getting Nicole wet again, he can see how hungry she is and that makes it nice for him to eat.

Nicole slips in and out of consciousness, mostly out. She knows that Seamus is there but has to fight will all her energy just to hold her eyes open. Sometimes she opens her eyes and sees nothing but rainbows. She can hear him moving about and tries to move. She thinks he must of tightened the ropes because without moving the rope is cutting further and further into her skin. She hurts and can think of nothing else except ending the pain. She dreams of cheeseburgers, french-fries, and water. She imagines painting a warm fire and bundling up tight in front of the TV. She feels happy for a moment but then feels a sharp pain that brings her into consciousness long enough to realize that he is spraying more cold water on her. She can't move away and can barely make out his figure but she can tell he is laughing and skipping around as he tortures her. She feels lost, alone, and out of control. She feels empty and he has succeeded in his plan. She thinks to herself that he has won and then slips back into a dream of rainbows and pots of gold.

"It is amazing how even the toughest of women fall when they are faced with the torment that they give to others," Seamus says into the air expecting no response.

"Look at you now, all puffed up and different colors, you think everyone will still love you now? You think you can still leave that boyfriend heartbroken while you hurt someone else? Well, it is a good thing I came along to take care of you. I won't let you hurt anyone else. Although they are looking for you, I am sure they will not find you in time, I picked this town for a reason … it has more places and secluded areas to hide than it has of anything else. This is an up and coming town that I have saved from you."

Seamus continues to clean making sure to remove any possible tie to him. He needed it to appear that she was there by herself. He packed everything up and used bleach over all the surfaces he could find and as a last minute thought decided to use it on Nicole as well. He dumped the remainder of the bottle over her as he removed the ropes. She screamed in response to the bleach touching her skin and then her open wounds where the rope had been. She could not move herself and he played with her discolored fingers and toes seeing how easily they could break. The easier they break the more frozen they are he thought to himself. He would not normally mess with her hands but he was mad at her about the search party. He was mad that he had to miss his favorite parts. He broke two fingers on each hand and a few toes enjoying the screams that came muffled through from Nicole. He could not imagine why he had not done this before, it was fun. He would have to remember in the future to add this to the punishment. He finished up and said goodbye to the beaten body that lay limp. He headed to the police station since it was already morning he knew people would be there to get assignments on where to search.

"You better hope that they do not choose to search here first or your death will be more painful for you and me, I just want you to die on your own… suffering in your punishment. I will see you soon," he pats her head as he stands to leave.

He arrives at the police station and hangs out in the back waiting for direction, there is a sign in sheet and he signs in as Nick Star it seemed creative to him. Nick for Nicole and Star short for starving. This thought makes him smile.

"Don't I know you?" Adria is peering into Seamus's smiling face.

"I don't think so."

"Sure, you were in the store. My friend and I wondered if we would see you again."

"Ok."

"So you are here to help find Nicole that is nice," Jillian jumps in trying to see who her friend is talking to.

"I saw the news and thought maybe I could help."

"Did you know Nicole?"

"No, but I had a sister that went missing when I was little and I know my parents wanted help so I thought I would help these parents."

"Did you find your sister?" Sara asks concerned.

"Oh, yes thanks to all the people in the community

who came and helped. That is why I am trying to do the same."

"Sounds good, we can use all the help we can get, they are sending search parties out to many different locations," Justin says while slapping Seamus's shoulder in a male way of saying, "your ok".

The girls fall back a little while snickering about how cute Seamus is and how old they think he is. Jillian asks for his name and he offers his hand and the name Nick. She takes it and gives him a rundown of everyone's names. He holds her hand for a second longer than normal wishing she could be his next and that he did not need to move onto a new place.

Ryan walks up to sign in as the conversation is ending and is a little more suspicious than anyone else of this Nick guy. "Hey, you said you live here, what do you do? I don't think I have seen you before."

"You probably haven't I do not get out much, I work from home. Internet stuff. I come out for a movie or to go to the store and such."

"Ok. What kind of internet stuff?"

"Dude, shut up," Justin snaps at Ryan not because the question is too intrusive but because he does not want to hear him talk.

They all break up as the FBI walks into the crowd assigning places to search. Seamus ends up in a group with a few police officers, but they all seem more absorbed in the fact they have to take orders from the FBI than concerned with who is in the group so he is not worried at all. The search begins.

Agent Fisher makes sure that only the site that the group is assigned to search is the one they know about. This poses a problem for Seamus. All the groups pile into different police vans and are on their way. Seamus spends the entire ride asking questions trying to find out where everyone is searching. The officers are primarily ignoring him and focusing on complaining to each other about the FBI overrunning their station. Seamus is starting to feel a little panic but tells himself to stay calm until he reaches their destination and then he can press harder.

Agent Fishers team is traveling in two separate groups but not in the community search parties. Agent Burke was able to narrow the search areas down significantly by adding in common factors from the last few victims. He used things such as the closeness of a store for supplies, areas that noise can carry, and the newness of the secluded area. Agent Carr's analysis of the killer also added to the factors, that he would want to feel at home and he would want the body found once he was done with it. That excluded personal storage facilities, warehouses that were closed down and left more of the new development areas. There were numerous new housing and industrial developments to search so Agent Vickers had began checking in with every sites managing team and discussing the progression of the projects. He asked questions like when the last work was completed, how long they had been away from the area, if they had an outside security company on site that watched all of the supplies left there. Most of the industrial buildings had security that walked the area every hour, although some of the guards came to admit they slept in their cars throughout the shift. They did walk the area at the beginning of shift and at the end. The housing developments did not seem to be as careful. Some of them had security but not more than a few and they did not check every house being completed, they just drove through the development keeping an eye out for kids partying or big trucks that could take supplies off site. Most of those security guards admitted that it was what they called a "dead man's site" so they read a book or slept in the car and rarely made any rounds. Agent Burke took all this information and plugged it into a computer program that gave him a smaller list of places to search. The team split into two and split the list. The more frequented areas they gave to the police officers to search with the people that showed up and they kept those that were most likely to house the victim. Agents Fisher, Burke, and Vickers went together and Agents Carr and Dalton went together. They split the list and headed out.

Meanwhile Seamus was arriving at an industrial building site close to other warehouses with the rest of his assigned group. He started pestering the most agitated officers as soon as they got out of the van. He figures he can use the frustration the officers had for the FBI agents to find out where the FBI team was and where they were searching.

"Hey, I could not help but overhear in the van about those FBI guys. That sucks them telling you what to do as if they are better at this job than you or something," Seamus ventures.

"Yeah, tell me about it," the officer replies shortly with an angry look on his face.

"I think I would have to tell them to shove it. They aren't even out here with you searching are they? They are probably sitting on their butts back at the station..."

"No, they are searching sites on their own with their own teams. They expect us to do as they say and work closely with them and support them and they don't even join our teams."

"Did they at least tell you where they are searching? You know keep you in the loop, I would demand at least that."

"Nope, they kept everything one big secret as if our department couldn't handle the information, like we would leak it to the killer or something."

"Yeah, that is ridiculous. So you only get to know where you are searching?"

"Yep, each team knows their own search area and no others. They even warned us that our ass would be on the line if we communicated our locations over the radio."

"That really sucks, I feel for you man. I don't think I could handle someone telling me how to do my job."

"Yeah, what do you do?"

"Small internet site that sells things like lotions and bath stuff."

"Lots of women spend lots of money on that I bet."

"Yeah, I do okay. But the best part is that I am my own boss. If I were you I would already have demanded to know where the sites were and what was happening in my own office."

"Yeah, but that is not how it works, I like my job just not the politics that go with it."

"I can understand that, where are we looking here?" Seamus directs the conversation back towards the search and the group hoping now to ditch the officer.

"Everywhere, they apparently think she may be in some abandoned area where no one can hear her."

They are right, Seamus thinks to himself. He begins to worry that they are closer to finding her than he thought so he must get back to where she is. Not only must her punishment be completed but he must be sure that she cannot tell them who he is. Although, he thinks to himself, she is so far gone now that they may not be able to save her anyway. He walks with the officer he has been talking to back to the group and once the officer is back in conversation with his other officer buddies Seamus slides away from the group surveying his surrounding and devising his plan on how to get back to the station and his truck without drawing suspicion to himself.

While Seamus is trying to get back the two FBI

teams are searching as fast as they can, trying not to miss a single house in any of the new developments that Burke outlined as the most likely areas to find Nicole. The job is taking longer than any of them wanted it to and they are getting desperate for a break. Agent Fisher's group has taken one half of the city focusing on the outskirts where there would be little to no traffic and Agent Carr's group has taken the other half of the city. Agent Dalton seems to get angrier and angrier as time passes without finding Nicole. Carr seems more concerned with every minute that passes that they may have pushed too hard and that the killer may have already finished Nicole after the announcement on the news that night before. She only hopes that the killer stays in his same patterns and needs Nicole to die on her own.

Agent's Burke and Vickers seem confident that they will find Nicole based on the calculations that they had made. Fisher is trying to be supportive but he is beginning to worry. They are yelling Nicole's name as they run through each housing project knowing that she would be too weak to respond but hoping that she will anyway.

"Hey Kid, how many more areas are there for us to search?" Fish asks Burke.

"We have explored about half of our list, we should be able to finish them all by nightfall I think."

"We will, maybe we should split up at each site we can cover the area faster that way," Vickers offers.

"We have been split up," Fish responds.

"No I mean the three of us each go a different way not just Burke and I and then you on your own, each of us out on our own."

"I don't think so."

"Why not, Burke has had all the same training as me, he is new but he can handle it," Vickers is arguing to help Burke to stand on his own.

Fisher takes a long look towards Burke who has not added anything to the argument and nods his head signaling that they will split up as Vickers stated.

Agents Carr and Dalton were splitting up also but staying within a house or two of each other. They were yelling clear as they cleared each house and moved onto the next. They would jump in the car to head to the next site and race to where they would start searching again.

CHAPTER TWELVE
Thursday

———————— ◊ ————————

Nicole is still unconscious and barely hanging on to the slow pulse that proves she is still alive. She will not be able to hear the teams of people searching for her or know that they are trying to beat Seamus to her. She lays motionless on the floor, untied and free to leave. She is past the point that would allow her to move, rise and run. She is past the point of being able to think or dream in her unconsciousness, she is almost gone.

Seamus has managed to leave his group unnoticed and slip away to a bus stop that will drop him close to his truck. He is impatient and pacing as the bus pulls up. He climbs into a front seat leaning forward ready to exit as soon as he reaches his stop. Only 15 minutes pass before he is able to climb off the bus and onto the street just a few blocks from where he parked his truck. He began in a jog but after a few steps he is in a sprint back to the truck. He knew he had to hurry and she had to die today, whether her body quit or not. His mind was racing as he thought of different ways to kill Nicole. He has not had to finish it himself before and he was unsure of how to do it exactly. He kept coming back to one particular way of killing her. He thought there would be justice in cutting her heart out, since that is what she would have done to others if he had not have saved them. He had a hunting knife in the truck that would work it seemed more poetic than just strangling her or beating her head in. He decided that cutting out her heart was the only way to go he could even leave it on display as a message to the FBI agents that are looking for him. However, as exciting as all this seemed to him, he was a little sad at the fact that he is not able to watch her die like she should be and that he was not going to have another meal, sleep, or warm shower to enjoy until he found his next victim.

While Seamus is climbing in his truck to return to the site where Nicole lays Agent's Carr and Dalton arrive at the housing development where she is. They begin at the far corner of the most recent lot. The houses have no walls yet and are easy to search since they can see through from room to room. They run up and down the stairs yelling Nicole's name hoping to find her soon. There are clouds forming heavily in the sky adding a darkness that is making it harder to search. It will probably begin to storm before they are done and they both pull out flashlights as they continue from house to house. They are entering each house with gun drawn hoping to find the victim and prepared to find the killer.

Seamus is close by he has to circle through the empty development for safety once he gets there although he wants to go straight to her. He is only minutes away from the development when Agent Dalton approaches the first house on the street that Nicole is held in. Nicole is dying on the floor of the last house on that street, on the corner for easy access in and out for Seamus. Dalton yells clear for the first house and Carr is finishing up the second. They continue down the street in this pattern until Agent Carr arrives at the corner house and begins to enter. Agent Dalton is inside the house next door and hears a car forcing him to run outside and see who might be there. Seamus turns the corner seeing the FBI vehicle just in time to turn around before being seen. He decides to go the back way to the house and realizes that he will only have a few minutes to complete his punishment. He parks and begins to run towards the back of the house as Agent Carr is beginning to head upstairs to where Nicole's motionless body lies.

There is a window over where Nicole lays on the ground and as Agent Carr reaches the top step Seamus can see her from outside. He stops dead in his tracks and turns back towards his truck shaking his head in anger the entire way. Agent Carr walks to the left at the tops of the stairs and finds Nicole.

"Dalton, Dalton … get in here …" Agent Carr shouts as she desperately tries to find a pulse on Nicole. She still has her gun in hand and is surveying her surroundings in case the killer is still there. Dalton comes running up the stairs and rushes over to Carr.

"Have you cleared the entire house?"

"No. You clear, I'll call in a bus and Fish," Carr is referring to calling in an ambulance. First she calls in the ambulance and then calls Agent Fisher.

"Hey Fish, we got her."

"Is she alive?"

"Barely."

"And the killer?"

"Nowhere in sight, and the area looks clean, even smells like bleach."

"We will meet you at the hospital, do not let the victim out of your site in case the killer is still around waiting to finish her off."

"Got it, I will ride in with her and Dalton can follow me in the car."

"The whole block is clear and I can't find a single shoe print even," Dalton reappears. "Is she alive?"

"I know she does not look it but she has a pulse…she has a chance."

"Look at her hands, all her fingers are going the

wrong way. He must of broken them, he has not done that before has he?"

"No, he is definitely escalating. Luckily he did not just kill her last night."

"Hey, you said he needs to watch them die, if so then where is he?"

"Good question. I hear the sirens coming up the street canvas the area before meeting me at the hospital I will radio Fish and tell him we need the man power for the area, I can't imagine he has gone far."

"Alright," Dalton slips out as the paramedics enter and begin trying to save Nicole.

They are trying to move Nicole onto a board as carefully as possible knowing that if they move her too harshly that her heart could just stop. They move her onto a board and then try to take her downstairs, it takes some time but they are able to get her to the ambulance and put her onto a gurney. Once inside the ambulance Carr steps in watching as the ambulance team tries to remove the wet cloths on Nicole and replace it with warm blankets. They are all yelling different things at each other as they cut off Nicole's clothes they also attach a heated oxygen tank. They try to attach other tubes to medicate and hydrate Nicole but her puffy swollen skin will not give way to the needles that they are trying to put into her arms. They are afraid to force it while the vehicle is moving for fear of causing more damage or strain to an already fragile body.

Agent Carr blocks out all the shouting around her and focuses on the body in front of her, Nicole's body. She finds it hard to find the girl from all the photos she has seen in this motionless body and face in front of her. The face of this young girl in front of her is almost unrecognizable, she is bloated and puffy. Her features are discolored, purple, pink, even a hint of yellow. Her whole body looked like it was blown up and beat with a baseball bat like she was a balloon piñata. Carr searched Nicole's face for some sign of life while she listened to all the commotion around her. They were arguing over what to do next.

Nicole's pulse has dropped and is barely being read by the monitor they have attached to her. She seems to be fading. The driver is hollering towards the back of the ambulance the estimated time of arrival at the hospital every few moments it seems.

"ETA 2 minutes…"

"She may not make it two minutes …"

"She has to … keep the oxygen going and keep changing out the blankets … keep her warm, but do not warm her too fast."

"Come on, fight for me … two minutes … you can make it two minutes …"

They arrive at the hospital and before the ambulance even reaches a complete stop the back doors are flung open and arms are reaching in to help remove Nicole and move her into the hospital. With all the commotion

Agent Carr walks by Agent Fisher without seeing him. She is keeping her eyes the entire time on Nicole. Once Nicole is taken into a surgery room Carr is left to watch through a viewing window set up for medical students. She is determined not to leave Nicole unguarded in case the killer returns. Fisher finds Carr and they update each other, Fisher has already sent Agents Burke and Vickers to the site where they found the victim to help Agent Dalton gather information.

"He won't make this mistake again," Carr starts.

"Which mistake?" Fisher asks.

"He will kill the victim himself next time. He will speed up the process, he won't chance us finding the next one."

"Then we will have to find him before he takes the next one. If this victim makes it then maybe we can find out who he is."

"If … this girl has suffered so much and we don't know if she even knows anything. Has anyone informed her family?"

"The parents are on their way now. We did not tell them how she looks though. I am hoping to keep them away from her as long as possible until she starts to look somewhat normal again."

"This girl will never be normal again…"

"But she will be alive."

"If she fights through this."

"You stay with her and I will head off the parents."

"Ok," Carr leans against the window she is watching through and glues her eyes onto Nicole while Fisher exits to find the parents.

The doctors are calm but franticly moving around trying to save Nicole. There are nurses running in circles around the bed they moved Nicole onto and doctors each trying to focus on different things. They are connecting tubes, changing out hot blankets, keeping Nicole's head up at an angle all in an attempt to combat the hypothermia. They are also trying to hook up liquids with electrolytes to hydrate her and a sugary substance that functions like a feeding tube at the moment to get some sugar into her system to prevent the body from continuing to digest itself. It is hours before they are able to calmly leave the room and Carr cannot tell if the news is good or bad so she approaches the doctors as they come out of the room.

"Well, will she live?"

"She is in critical condition but I suspect after watching over her for the night she will be moved to stable. There is no telling how she will be when she wakes up or when she will wake up."

"Is she in a coma?"

"Yes, but we expect she will wake up eventually the question will remain to be whether or not she has brain function or not."

"So she may not be able to talk to us."

"She may not even remember who she is. Amnesia

is common in cases of trauma like this. Now if you will excuse me I have to talk to her family and get her assigned to a room."

"Thank you doctor," Carr turns back to watch the room.

Out in the waiting room Nicole's mom has fallen to the ground in tears and her father is holding her tight, tears running down his face. Nicole's friends are all there sitting quietly against the wall. The doctor tells them that they should go home and return the next day that they will not be able to see Nicole for a while. They nod and leave together each of them holding up one another. Once they left the parents asked if they could see Nicole.

"She does not look like the daughter you remember right now, but at this point I think it is safe to say that she looks worse than she is. I will have the nurse take you to her room once she is moved. Please remember we still have a way to go. In the morning we will try to reset the broken bones but right now I want to get her stable before we have to do any surgery or other trauma to her body."

"Thank you doctor, we understand," Nicole's dad looks up from his wife.

It is not long before the nurse is escorting Nicole's parents to her bedside and they meet Agent Carr. They are thankful to Agent Carr for finding their daughter but uncomfortable that she is still there. To them this means that their daughter is still in danger. They are right, she is still in danger.

Chapter Thirteen
Friday

———— ◊ ————

Seamus is driving around town aimlessly, he knows that he should have left town already and moved on to the next victim but the fact that this one is sitting in the hospital with hopes of returning to her life prevents him from leaving. He needs to finish this one, he has to find a way into the hospital room and maybe just smother her to death. The news said she is in critical condition so it should be pretty easy. It will be the security and the parents to worry about. As he circles through the parking lot he spots the group of friends that he spoke to the previous morning before the search. That can be his way in to get the information he needs. He parks near where they are walking and waves them down.

"Hey there, I see we had the same idea," Seamus shouts.

"Hello Nick. Why are you here?" Adria asks.

"Well, on the news they said your friend was here and I just wanted to see how she is and they will not say to anyone other than family."

"That's sweet," Sara says with a smile.

"Or creepy ... sorry man, it's just that we don't know you and it's a kinda hard time right now we could use the space. Thanks for your help looking though," Justin butts in.

"Sorry, I understand. I just wanted to be sure she was okay. I remember how it was for my family," Seamus says with his arms up showing he is not trying to make trouble.

"Well, she is not awake and they don't know if she will wake up today. We don't even know if they will let us see her today we are just here for support," Adria says while Jillian gives her a hard look meaning shut up.

"Thank you. I am glad that she has so many friends to help her she is going to need you all. I will be on my way now," Seamus tipped his head in a nod of goodbye and headed back to his truck. He drove around to the back of the hospital where some of the employees entered and watched for the rest of the day, devising a plan to get into the hospital and into Nicole's room.

The cleaning service and the uniform service both entered and exited through the back of the building.

He just needed to decide if wanted confrontation or to find another way. Confrontation would give him limited time in the hospital he wanted to take his time, learn the layout of the hospital and wait until the middle of night when the exhausted parents would go home or be asleep in the room and there would be a smaller hospital staff. He decided that he needed to get in during the day and hide out until nightfall. While he is planning this out in his mind the delivery guy for uniforms enters the building and leaves the back of the truck open, too perfect.

Seamus runs up to the truck and quickly takes a uniform including a hat and mask to hide his face and runs back to the truck. He drives the truck down the street and hides it from view around a corner. He walks to the back entrance and waits until the group having a cigarette start heading back inside and mixes in with the group in order to use their badge to enter the building. Once inside he starts looking around making sure to blend when he needed to and hide when he needed to. He couldn't help but think to himself that this is a little fun, a cat and mouse game in an obstacle course.

"She is doing better this morning but I would like to wait another day before we try to do anything else." The doctor is speaking to the parents as Seamus walks by.

"We understand," Nicole's father says.

"You two really should go and get something to eat and get some sleep maybe you can switch off who stays here and who goes home."

"We don't want to leave until our little girl wakes up," Nicole's mother answers.

"Alright, well at least go down to the cafeteria and get something to eat and drink, Agent Carr will still be here with your daughter and she can send a nurse for you if anything changes."

Shit, Seamus thinks to himself, there is an agent in there. He has to find a way to draw the agent out of the room long enough to finish the job. Maybe he can find a syringe and a drug to cause an overdose. Or maybe just a large air bubble that will travel to her heart through her blood, but then he has to be sure to get the appropriate vein. He will look for a drug and wait until the agent uses the restroom he may have to dose the parents as well but that will be Nicole's fault for not dying with him like she was suppose to.

While Seamus looked for his lethal cocktail Nicole's parents insisted that Agent Carr take a break if they were going to. So Carr called Fisher and asked him to send Dalton over to stand guard while she took a nap and ate some food. Once Agent Dalton arrived Agent Carr and Nicole's parents all left the room for a break. Carr went to lie down on one of the doctor's bunk beds where they grab some sleep between hectic shift work. The parents went to eat in the cafeteria. Seamus found the supplies he needed and returned to Nicole's room where he at first did not see Agent Dalton who had positioned himself in a chair adjacent to the doorway inside the room.

He caught a glimpse of him as he started to enter and pulled himself back and headed to the room next door anticipating his next move. He thought about acting like a nurse and administering the shot but his uniform was wrong for that. He was undecided as to what to do so he waited staring at the wall as if he could see Nicole right through it.

Agent Dalton sat reading a book not even noticing that someone had started to enter the room. He was calm and collected but bored. He was used to running down the bad guy not babysitting the victim and it was a little unsettling to him to have to watch this victim. He became used to seeing dead bodies and dealing with crazy people in his job but it was a rare to save someone and have to guard them. He felt bad for this victim more than he normally did. He knew this victim's nightmare would never be over, she would have to deal with it over and over again throughout her life. He sat staring at her unknowing that in the next room was the killer trying to stare at her too.

The parents returned and decided the doctor was right they needed to be strong for their daughter when she woke up so they needed to sleep. They were going to go home for a few hours and wanted to be sure that Agent Dalton had the necessary information to contact them. They said their goodbyes to Nicole and Dalton and headed home promising to return before nightfall. They did not want their daughter spending the night alone without them.

Once the parents left Seamus started thinking of ways to draw the agent out of the room. He decided that a distraction was the best way to do that, so he set a plan into motion and began creating a distraction.

The nurse's station was not far from Nicole's room and it would be best place for the plan to take place. It is close enough that the agent would feel safe leaving Nicole's room but far enough that Seamus could sneak in while the agents back was turned. Seamus starting taking the nurse's things, agitating them and making it hard for them to do their jobs, he started with pens and then files, charts and stethoscopes. He watched them look frantically from one side of the station to the other for their things. Once they were all frustrated he put all the items into one area belonging to one of the nurses, to give the appearance that she had taken them, he even added some narcotics to sweeten the pot. It was only a short time as one of the nurses looked for a thermometer that she stumbled upon the stash and accusations began to be thrown. Seamus waited patiently as the argument turned louder and louder.

Agent Dalton was sitting and reading a magazine when the commotion started. He leans his head out the door to see what is happening while maintaining his hand on his gun, just in case. He can see the nurses are ready to have it out and he starts out of the room to help, looking back to be sure he can see the doorway to Nicole's room from the nurse's station. As he grabs one nurse to pull her away from another his head is down just long enough for Seamus to slip into Nicole's room.

Seamus approaches Nicole's body ready to complete his task. He does not like that they are reversing what he has done. She is even starting to look a little normal. He shakes his head and reaches for her arm starting to put the needle deep into her arm when he hears the Agent's footsteps returning to the room, he needs time to get out. He pushes slightly on the syringe but only the tiniest amount seeps out and into Nicole before he is out the door and back in the room next door. He waits for the next commotion to leave he waits for only a moment.

"Close down the hospital now!" Agent Dalton is yelling into his radio, gun drawn. "He is here. I am telling you he is here."

"Is she ok?" A nurse comes running into the room.

"You tell me. I see a heartbeat but what's in that needle?"

"I don't know… her vitals are ok. I will get the doctor," the nurse exits the room holding the needle out away from her as if it were a dirty diaper.

"Alright," Dalton gets onto his phone with Fisher. "He is here, he tried to put a needle in her arm."

"A needle of what? And where the hell were you?"

"There was a fight and I …"

"Say no more. I am on my way there now, notify Carr to return to the room, I want two sets of eyes on her right now."

As the doctor enters the room Dalton is standing over Nicole trying to see if she is ok. The doctor starts checking the machines and then turns to Nicole and jumps back. Nicole's eyes are open and looking around. She is making no other movement but she is awake. The doctor is shocked and Dalton is already on the phone to the parents and then to Fisher. He tells the doctor that he is locking down the room and only the parents are allowed in, no other friends or family. Seconds later, Agent Carr enters the room.

"She's awake? How?" Carr asks looking confused.

"I am not sure, she shouldn't be yet, maybe whatever that needle had in it rattled her awake. I have no idea without knowing what was in the needle," the doctor responds.

"Her parents," Carr looks to Dalton.

"Already called them and they are on their way. I have Fisher and the police locking down the hospital he has to still be here."

"Has she said anything?"

"No. She literally just opened her eyes right before you walked in."

"Nicole, I am Agent Carr I am here to help you. Your parents are on their way, you are safe now."

Nicole stared blankly across the room and Carr began to worry that there may be permanent brain damage. She would have to wait for the doctors to decide that though.

Meanwhile downstairs the parents were entering the hospital as Seamus was planning his exit. The parents were practically running and he watched them as they stopped and told the friends that Nicole was awake. Once Seamus heard this he knew it was probably too late. He would stick around though as long as possible to see if they dropped their guard long enough. He slid into a storage room and made his way into the ceiling and stayed still waiting.

Nicole's parents entered the room and headed straight for their daughter not knowing that they almost lost her, again. They were at her side and kissing her face before anyone could say a word. Nicole's eyes seemed to swell up a bit at the site of her parents and the doctor said the reaction was extraordinary. They continued talking to Nicole without a response until her eyes fell shut again. The doctor reassured them all that Nicole would awake again that she was tired and that her body worked best to repair itself when resting and to let her sleep. They let her rest but they all stayed in the room unwilling to leave for the chance of something happening again.

Throughout the evening and the night the officers searched the hospital and everyone who came and went. Agent Fisher moved his team to the hospital and began working out of one of the hospitals conference rooms. The team is determined to protect Nicole and to catch the killer they have been tracking before he kills again.

"Did you find anything new to figure out who this

guy is?" Fisher is addressing Burke who is plugging away on his computer.

"I keep running across the same information over and over. We need something new."

"Maybe we will get something from the lab once they finishing processing the location and the victim."

"Until then I'll keep plugging away."

"Good, and the team will continue to check the hospital and watch the room. Call us if you need anything from us."

"Will do."

CHAPTER FOURTEEN
Monday

———— ◊ ————

A few days have passed and the hospital is still bustling with police officers watching and searching the people coming and going. There has been no sign of the killer and the FBI team is feeling quite frustrated. Nicole's friends and family have been at the hospital everyday but today is the first day the friends will be able to actually see Nicole. Nicole has been upgraded to stable condition and they have preformed a small surgery to repair her hands and feet as much as possible. The doctors think Nicole's recovery so far has been amazing and are excited to see if she continues to heal and progress at such a fast rate.

In Nicole's room she is just waking up for the day and her mother is at her side holding her bandaged hand. Her father is sitting in a chair leaning towards the bed.

They both look very tired and yet seem happy to see their daughter is awake again.

"How are you this morning," her mother is looking into her eyes hoping to see some kind of response since Nicole still has not spoken to them.

"You look beautiful this morning," her mother adds.

"Where ... am I?" Nicole stutters.

Her father jumps to his feet and to her bedside, while her mother leans her head back towards the door asking Agent Carr to alert a nurse.

"Honey, you are in the hospital," her father answers.

"Why?" Nicole's voice is quite hoarse and hard to hear but seems to be getting stronger by the moment.

"Well, there was ... well ... I ..." her mother cannot seem to get out the words to tell her daughter what she has been through and is not sure she wants to.

"Mom ..."

"Yes?"

"My hands?" As Nicole raises her hands she chokes on the question.

Tears form in her mother's eyes and she looks to Agent Carr for help in explaining things to her daughter. In that moment the doctor walks into the room having heard Carr yelling for the nurses. He is surprised to hear that Nicole has began talking and urges them not to pressure her to talk too much.

"Hello Nicole, I am Dr. Geiser and I have been treating you since you came in."

"When did I …"

"Well, what is the last thing that you remember Nicole?"

"History class … Aaron told me he got into Stanford."

"What day was that?"

"It's Friday … the 8th."

"It is actually Monday … the 18th."

"What … how?"

"I will let Agent Carr help you with that, but for now I really wish you would rest for a while. You have some friends in the waiting room that would like to visit with you this afternoon."

"Who's Agent … why they here?" Nicole is straining a bit to talk.

"I am Agent Carr and I will explain everything if you give me about an hour of rest first, I will bring in my boss and we will talk to you then," Agent Carr says stepping towards the hospital bed.

"Ok," Nicole mutters, she is tired and closes her eyes to rest a bit feeling very confused.

Meanwhile, Seamus is still in the hospital popping in and out of different areas trying to gain information on Nicole and the status of the FBI unit. He hopes they will leave once she is doing is better and before she can tell them anything. He hears from the nurses that she is recovering quickly and this upsets him. He needs more information so he decides to run into the friends in the waiting room. He waits until they have talked to the parents and the parents leave. He has left his uniform in the ceiling of the stockroom and looks like any other guy. He approaches from behind the group so they cannot see that he has come from within the hospital.

"Hey, how are things going with your friend?" He addresses the girls.

"Hey, you again huh?" Adria answers.

"Yeah, I have an appointment today and saw you all over here, thought I would ask how she was doing ..."

"She is better, stable. She even talked this morning."

"You don't say? Have you seen her yet?"

"No, we are going to be able to see her this afternoon she is resting now."

"Well, that is good news. They are probably keeping you down here so the police can talk to her first."

"No. She doesn't remember anything about the last week or so her mom said," Sarah adds wanting to be apart of the conversation.

"Well, that can happen I guess. I hope she feels better but I have to run I do not want to be late for my appointment."

"Sure, see you later," Adria and Sarah say together while Jillian sits shaking her head.

Seamus walks off in the direction of the elevators but takes a detour at the information desk. He is comfortable now in leaving since she cannot remember him. Besides several days have passed and he has not eaten, slept or showered. He needs to find a new girl quick so that he can survive. He waits for the police officers to become distracted with a woman they are talking to and slips out the exit. He heads to his truck and starts thinking of which way to head, he will need to create some space between himself and this FBI team tracking him. He climbs into his truck and settles in, ready to move on to teach his next lesson.

In the waiting room the friends are all talking about what to say to Nicole. They are unsure of what to say other than feel better and happy to see you. Justin seems uncomfortable and the girls are nervous. Jillian sits patiently waiting to see how her best friend is not sure of what to expect. Justin finally breaks the silence, asking, "they said she looks different, how bad do you think it is?"

"Looks aren't everything you know," Adria snaps at Justin before Jillian has the chance.

"No, I mean I hope she does not look like she is in pain. I don't know how to handle her in pain."

"Oh, I don't know, I'm more worried about to what to say …" Adria says.

"Just talk to her like nothing happened … tell her about art class and the basketball game," Jillian says.

"Even though she can't remember anything?" Sarah asks.

"I don't know just don't treat her bad she is going to want to feel normal I am sure," Jill tries to explain.

"Alright," they all agree.

Upstairs the time has passed by and Agent Fisher and Agent Carr await Nicole's awakening. It has been almost two hours since Carr promised to explain things to Nicole and she was there waiting to stand by that promise. When Nicole finally awakes she does not say anything at first she is looking around the room and at her hands covered in bandages. Finally she looks to Agent Carr and raises her hand up.

"What's wrong with them?"

"Your fingers were broken and some suffer from frostbite."

"Do they work?"

"We are not sure yet, you will be able to try them in a few weeks."

"Was I in an accident?"

"No, you were kidnapped and held by someone we are looking for."

"By who?"

"We don't know, we were hoping you could help us with that."

"Why don't I remember?"

"That is more the doctor's area of expertise but from what has been explained to us it is common to have some amnesia associated with hypothermia. There is also the idea that what you experienced was so horrible that your mind decided to block it out."

"Will it come back?"

"I don't know."

"You said hypothermia, what happened to me?"

"We are not sure, we know that you had hypothermia and were suffering from starvation when we found you as well as the broken fingers and toes."

"When was I taken? From where?"

"We think on the way home from a party, you were walking home in the middle of the night."

"What party? Why don't I remember a party?"

"They are not sure, memory loss is a funny thing and there is no way to predict it and no way to know when or if it will return."

"Who found me?"

"My partner and I physically found you but there were a lot of people looking for you, your family and friends and community."

"Was I suppose to die?"

"No one is suppose to die like that."

"Has he killed before?"

"Yes."

"Will he kill again?"

"Yes."

"Can you catch him?"

"Yes."

"But you need me to tell you something that is why you stayed here in my room?"

"We are hoping for something yes, but primarily we stayed because we wanted to make sure you were safe."

"You think he will try to get me still?"

"We don't know… he has never been interrupted before."

"Do my friends know what happened to me?"

"Yes, and no. They know that you were starved and such but they do not know about your hands or anything else."

"What is anything else?"

"You looked very different when we found you, you look more normal now but hypothermia and starvation both cause swelling and discoloration. You have normal color skin now and most of the swelling has went down, but not all of it. Also, you have some un-repairable nerve damage in your feet from frost bite. You will have to have physical therapy to learn to walk again."

At this last statement Nicole starts to pull at the covers with her bandaged hands, she wants to see her feet but cannot move the covers. Her mother helps her while tears stream down her face. Nicole herself begins to cry at the site of her own swollen legs and discolored feet, she tries to move her toes and a few move a little but she does not feel it. The tips of some of her toes are black and blue and look dead, her feet though swollen do not look far from normal. She asks why she cannot feel the toes.

"Frostbite has killed some of the tissue in your toes, when we first found you your feet were almost all black and blue and they were afraid they would have to amputate them. Luckily, there are some very resourceful and intelligent doctors here who managed to save most of your feet and hands."

"My fingers are the same way?"

"Yes, but they have already done one surgery that included removing some dead tissue. A few of your fingers will be shorter than the others and they will do the same to your feet once you are a little stronger."

"How do you know so much? Medically I mean?"

"I don't. I am just doing my job, and right now my job is you."

Nicole looks up to her mother and demands to see a mirror. Nicole's mother reluctantly hands the mirror to her hoping that Nicole will realize how lucky she is and how much worse it could have been. Nicole makes no expression at first and actually seems calmed looking into the mirror. She turns her head left to right a couple times and then puts the mirror face down against her stomach.

"It is not that bad. After seeing my feet I was afraid that my face would be blue and black and look dead."

"They saved your nose but you do have some dead tissue on one of your ears, but that is ok, you are still beautiful," Nicole's father wanted to reassure his daughter.

"Ok. So what is next?" Nicole asks with a glazed tired look in her eyes.

"You rest and in a couple weeks they will be able to start some rehabilitation with you they believe."

"Alright, I have more questions but right now I want to sleep."

"Then sleep honey, we will be here when you wake up," her mother says comfortingly.

Nicole fades into sleep and Agent Fisher pulls Agent Carr into the hallway. He is searching her face as he asks his first question.

"Are you getting too close to this case?"

"Wanting to do my job, protect the victim and catch the criminal, means I have to get a little close. I am not getting too close," Carr stands her ground.

"Ok. Then I want you to continue to talk with our victim be supportive and be someone she can trust if anything comes back to her that can help us. We will move back to the police station and set up there until we get something more. I will send you relief but stay close to the family and still honor the risk that our killer may not have moved on."

"Alright, I will keep you posted as to anything that develops with the victim."

"Thank you. I will talk to you soon." With the thank you Agent Fisher turns and heads away from Agent Carr down the hallway.

Nicole sleeps for few hours before waking and eating. She cannot really seem to taste the food but she is happy to be able to eat some food on her own and not just through a tube. She has cottage cheese and mashed potatoes and other soft things that she asked for. While she is eating her mother asks if she is up to seeing her friends, it is evening now and they have waited all day downstairs to see her. At first she is reluctant but feels bad they have been waiting and agrees to have them come up.

Jillian is the first to enter the room while the others stay in the hallway. She takes a deep breath as she walks in finding it difficult to see her friend in the hospital bed with all the machines. She walks over to the bed wanting to hug her friend but scared that she will hurt her if she does so she just stands awkwardly next to the bed and smiles down at her friend.

"It is so good to see you," Jillian starts.

"Ok, Jill. I know I look like crap but it is me and you, best friends."

They both are tearing up but have silly smiles shinning out from under the tears. Jillian makes a heavy sighing sound and offers her hand to Nicole's arm.

"I really am glad to see you. I was lost without you while you were … well …gone."

"I am glad to see you too. It is a little different for me. I don't remember being gone. It feels like no time past although I feel like I was ran over by a semi truck."

"Well, luckily you don't look ran over," Jillian is finding comfort in her friend and is able to joke a little.

"Yeah, I look great," Nicole jokes rolling her eyes. She really is happy to have Jillian there with her.

"I wanted you to know that I am sorry…"

"Why are you sorry you didn't run me over …"

"No, the night that you went missing I should have given you a ride or something … all of us feel horrible about it."

"I don't remember … why would I need a ride?"

"You were well it doesn't matter I love you and I am happy you are ok," Jillian is unsure of how much she is suppose to talk about.

"You will have to do better than that. I am gonna be here for a while I hope you will come and visit and fill me in on the stuff you remember that I do not?" Nicole asks.

"Of course I will be here with you. I am not spending any more time away from my best friend than I have to," they smile at each other.

"So the girls are here … and Justin … who do you want me to send in first?" Jillian asks.

"Send everyone in …"

"They told us only one or two at a time."

"I don't care what they say I want to see everyone squeeze into this little room and I am the one stuck here so I make the rules," Nicole is smiling as she says this but is quite serious. She does not want to see Justin by herself and she feels almost normal with friends there.

"You're the boss. I will get them," Jillian is gone and back in seconds.

"School sucks without you there," Sarah blurts out as soon as she lays eyes on Nicole.

"She's right, we miss you," Adria says.

"Have you two been being good?" Nicole teases them.

"Yes," they say in unison with an exasperated expression as if to say how could she even think they would be bad.

"Hi Babe. I missed you, I am glad you are ok," Justin interjects he is standing at the end of Nicole's bed but has made no effort to move closer to her.

"Thank you. I am glad you are here," Nicole feels detached from Justin but is unsure as to why.

"So what is going on at school? How's the basketball team doing? How is Art Class?" Nicole looks around the room to all of them and they all begin filling her in on the everyday things happening at school since she has been gone. She likes listening to the gossip and Justin referring to her friends as the three musketeers, she feels at home even though she is stuck in a hospital bed. It is not long before she is getting tired and her parents are pushing the friends to leave. Nicole asks for Justin to stay behind for a second but give warm smiles to the girls as they leave. He approaches her bed near her head, closer than he had been the entire time in the room.

"Justin, I don't know why and I don't know if it will change but I wanted to tell you not to come see me."

"Why? I want to see you, I love you Nicole."

"And I love you too. But I think I have a long round ahead with things like rehab and I don't want to worry about whether you are here out of love or obligation. If when I am better we want to make it work then we will. Right now, I want friends to support me and help me feel normal where I otherwise do not. Right now, I want don't want to be attached to anyone. I hope you understand, you have been my best friend for years and I hope we can get back to being friends."

"If that is what you want then I will honor that but I do want to see you and I do support you. I will not pressure you. I will just visit as a friend someone to bring some perspective to the gossip the girls will bring."

"That would be fine. If you are going to come back can you do me a favor and talk to Aaron from my history class, ask him if he got into Stanford."

"Dorky Aaron?"

"Yes, please the last thing I remember is him telling me he got into Stanford but it is fuzzy. I just need to know if it is a real memory or not."

"Alright will do. I will call the room here once I find out at school tomorrow."

"Thank you, for everything Justin, for understanding."

Justin smiles down at her and lays his hand on her arm to say goodbye. She starts to pull away without knowing why. She looks away and Justin leaves. She decides to rest since her body aches and she can't really move much.

CHAPTER FIFTEEN
Three Weeks Later

———— ◊ ————

Three weeks have passed since Nicole first woke up in the hospital bed and today she gets to take the bandages off of her hands and see how much her hands have healed. She is anxious and nervous at the same time. She is afraid of how bad they will be and also excited to get her hands back. She is sitting up in the raised bed she does not get as tired lately. She has not remembered anything new but her body has been healing and she has even been outside once in a wheelchair. Her mother is standing beside the bed when the doctor walks in.

"Good afternoon doctor," Nicole's mother starts.

"Good afternoon how is our patient today?"

"She is ready to see her hands again ..." Nicole interjects.

"Well, let's remove those bandages and see what we have then. Remember they will still be swollen and such so they will still look a little worse than they will once you start rehabilitating them."

"Alright. Let's do it," Nicole doesn't want to wait anymore.

The doctor puts Nicole's right hand into a wash bin and cuts away the bandage. Once the bandage is removed he pours warm water over the hand allowing it to soak for a minute before instructing the nurse to check the stitches while he starts the other hand. Everyone in the room is silent as they go through the process of checking Nicole's hands. They are puffy and bruised but there is not too much frostbite that is still visible. As the doctor finishes he seems satisfied with the progress the hands have made. Nicole begins inspecting her hands while her parents discuss the next thing to do for Nicole with the doctor. All this time Agent Carr has stayed in the corner of the room hopeful for Nicole. Nicole turns her head towards the agent and asks what she thinks.

"Agent Carr, what do you think? My parents will sugar coat it so please tell me what you think."

"I told you, call me Rhonda. I think that the doctor is right to be satisfied with the job he did. He saved most of your hands and fingers and they seem to be healing miraculously. I am not going to lie though I know they are not the same and will never be the same but they saved your hands, that is awfully lucky."

"Thank you, Rhonda. I think you are right. I am lucky to still have my hands and my life as you have helped me to understand."

"You have made it very easy you are quite the mature young lady with a good strong head on your shoulders."

Nicole's parents stood with the doctor smiling at the compliment just bestowed upon their daughter but Agent Carr. Nicole continued to analyze her hands seeing that a few were shorter than the others where they had surgically removed the tips where there was dead tissue. Her fingers looked a little crooked also and there were several areas where stitches were showing.

"When can we take the stitches out and start doing work to strengthen my hands again?"

"Well. I want to leave the stitches in for another week or so we will monitor your progress and see, you can do small things with your hands now but try to keep them immobile most of the day. You can start physical therapy in about another two weeks. By having them out in the open without bandages it should help with some swelling and make them easier to monitor. If you use them too much though I will be forced to bandage them back up to heal, understand?"

"I do doctor, thank you."

A nurse enters the room and asks if Nicole's parents can come outside for a minute so they do, returning a moment later to ask Nicole if she up to seeing a visitor.

They do not recognize the boy but he says that he knows Nicole.

"Honey, there is a Ryan here to see you …"

"Ryan, who?"

"This is funny, he says he is Romeo to your Juliet?" her father kind of laughs as he says this.

"Oh yeah, ok." Nicole is a little nervous at seeing Ryan, Jillian filled her in on the details of their kiss at the party and she is a little embarrassed about both the behavior and not remembering. Ryan enters the room with flowers and a gift box.

"Hello Nicole, I know that you don't really remember me much but I had to come see you," Ryan starts in right away like an excited child.

"I remember you in general from school but everything else has been told to me second hand by the girls and I can't be sure how reliable they are."

"Well, I have been talking to your friend Jillian and she told me that you were getting the bandages off your hands today. I remember you telling me about getting into a big art school so I thought I would bring you a Present." As he says this he opens the tops of the gift box and pulls out an artist sketchpad and a package of pencils, both traditional and colored pencils.

"I don't know what to say."

"Just say I can keep coming to see you. I told you the night that you went missing that you were amazing and I think that is even more true now."

"What do you mean?" Nicole is unsure of how to take some of things he is saying.

"You went through a horrible thing and yet here you are, you are a strong person and I believe filled with talents. I would be honored to be your friend and maybe someday more."

"I feel like I am being pranked or something, no offense."

"None taken. Jillian warned me that you were a little more down to earth and how hard it would be since you would not remember me. She also told me you do not want a boyfriend, just friends for right now so I am offering my friendship."

"I appreciate that and the gift. I have felt like a part of me was missing since I could not practice my art. I am not sure if I will ever be any good again ..." Nicole lets the sentence fall into the air as she fights back tears.

"You will be great again, I know it," Ryan placed his hand on her arm and although she flinched a little his hand remained and he did not get offended by it.

"I will have to find out how soon I can start to draw again. I appreciate everything from you Ryan and I am happy to call you my friend."

They continued talking for a while before the nurse came in shooing him out telling him he can come back tomorrow but that Nicole needed her rest. Agent Carr told Nicole that she too would be leaving for the evening and to call if she needed anything since she would be close by. The team had stopped staying around the clock but made sure that someone was with Nicole anytime they were not. There had been nothing new from the killer they chased but they knew if he was alive out there he would surface again. Before Agent Carr exited into the hallway she turned back to Nicole and smiled.

"Hey, I like that one, he's a keeper," and with a wink she was off.

The next morning Nicole got the ok from the doctor to try to draw but for no more than a half hour at a time he warned or he would take the pad away. At first Nicole could not even control her fingers around the pencil and then every line was shaky but it would not be long before she would be drawing beautiful pictures again.

Chapter Sixteen
Seamus

———— ◊ ————

The day is ending and Seamus is driving along watching everyone on the streets that he passes. He is looking for the next one he will punish. He made it through the past three weeks only by picking up a prostitute, he punished her. It was not as satisfying as the young ladies he normally punishes but he knew he needed to stay low for a while and he also needed to sleep and eat to survive. He could not do that without someone being hungry and cold. He took his time with the prostitute and practiced different forms of punishment on her. She was unimportant, just a dirty hooker. He knew now that he enjoyed adding pain like he had with Nicole when he broke her fingers and toes. He found better ways of adding pain though and he was eager to try them on his next young victim. He still let the hooker die on her own and he would continue to do that. He is not the executioner he is only the punisher, the teacher.

There is a group of teenage girls that has come to the same coffee shop to hangout for the last three nights. Seamus is watching them waiting to see if any of them split from the group, they all fit his type but two in particular stand out to him. They are the ones that the young boys approach that are sent away as they laugh. They are perfect for his teachings. He waits and watches debating in his mind if he could take both of them. He could probably get away with teaching two at once but it would be like having a school instead of just an individual tutoring session. He thinks of how he could do it while he watches them laughing and flirting.

The girls that Seamus is watching are local cheerleaders, they are seniors at the high school nearby and they all go out for mochas after practice, they have no idea they are being watched. They continue to hang out as he watches until one of them starts arguing with another as teenage girls tend to do. The one left alone is one of the ones that Seamus wants and he is excited once he sees his opportunity forming. The girls separate and walk to their cars. The one he wants stays back and cleans off the table the girls had been sitting at. He moves his truck to the parking lot of the coffee shop debating on following her first or taking her there. An abandoned car would draw attention too soon he would wait until she drove home and take her before she enters her house. So he waits until she is in her car and then follows her. He stays far enough back not to gain attention.

The girl parks on the street in front of her house since her parents are parked in the driveway. She is getting out of the car as he parks across the street but she does not even notice him. She steps onto the front lawn to cross it as his hand covers her mouth. She drops her backpack and he scoops it up dragging her kicking to the truck. Once inside the truck one swift hit across the back of the head with a wrench and she is out. He smiles and drives away, he has already picked out a spot for her.

Meanwhile the FBI team feels hopeless and has run out of ideas. They have also overstayed their welcome with the police department. Agent Fisher is considering moving on to a new case but both Agent Dalton and Agent Carr have been pressuring him not to give up.

"I think that without something new that by the end of the week we will have to pack up and head back to headquarters for our next assignment."

"We haven't finished this one. I am not letting this guy beat me," Dalton mutters to Fisher.

"We all feel that way but we are lost without a new lead."

"So you're saying if we want to catch this guy he has to do it again," Agent Vickers says.

"That or find me other bodies, I don't know I would

like to believe that we can catch him without it but we can't. That is just reality."

"He is right. Nicole is not remembering anything and the lab test have come back with the same things we already knew. We need something new." Agent Carr surrenders.

As the team discusses the problems they face and lack of possible solutions, Seamus is settling in with his next young victim. The parents of the girl he has taken already notified police that they think something has happened to their daughter. They found her keys in the front lawn at their home and car parked out front, but she never arrived home. They police department has told them to wait 24 hours and call back if she is still missing and they will file a report until then they assume she is just a teenager being a teenager.

Seamus is trying to decide which things to do first with his new victim. He thinks of all the things he wants to do but starts out the same. They must be puffy and weak for the best parts. He plans to use belts for lashings like children would get when they were bad before the government got involved and stopped teachers from disciplining their students. He had not forgotten how important punishment was, these girls could not learn without it and they are lucky that he has chosen them. In his mind he displaces the truth that one has gotten away. He is back in the peaceful place of his mind that allows him to enjoy the normal things in life while he teaches.

He taunts the girl he has until she finally tells him her name, Britney. She refuses to talk with him and he gets frustrated but he continues to tell her how much he is going to help her. How much she is going to learn and how she will never hurt anyone again.

"What are you talking about? Let me go …"

"Oh, now that is cute, you telling the teacher what to do."

"Teacher? You're crazy …"

"No. I am the only sane one left that is willing to do what needs to be done to stop people like you in this world, people who destroy others and never look back."

"Someone destroyed you," she mutters this angry statement but he takes it as a question.

"Yes, that is how I learned what you are like and came to realize what needed to be done. I am a hero now. I am saving people just like me."

"Fuck you."

Seamus smiles, she is feisty and he is going to have so much fun with her. Just watching her squirm around on the ground trying to get out of her restraints makes him giddy inside. He is a hero and someday everyone will know that.

He continues to watch her squirm while he enjoys an apple. He forgets how much he enjoys apples, how sweet they are until times like this. He still wants more though and that is a new feeling for him. For the longest time just watching was enough and now he feels like he needs a little more, like they need to be punished a little more. Maybe he is punishing them for Nicole getting away or maybe he is just getting better at his job, his role in teaching these girls. In truth he is escalating as a serial killer.

CHAPTER SEVENTEEN
Artwork

———— ◊ ————

A few days pass and Nicole continues to draw every chance she gets. She is getting better by leaps and bounds. Everyone tells her that it is because she has true artist talent. She is having one problem though the more she draws what is in her head the more confused she feels by the things in her mind. She has even started having odd dreams that scare her but she has not told anyone yet. She is sitting up in bed drawing when Ryan arrives with Jillian to visit for the day.

"Hey you're drawing," Jillian exclaims as she enters delighted to see her friend doing what she loves best.

"Trying to …" Nicole laughs.

"What'cha working on?" Ryan tries to sneak a peek.

"I am not sure just stuff in my head I guess."

"Hey these are really good. I wouldn't even know you were learning all over again."

"Yeah, she is a true artist, she is going to be just as good if not better than before," Jillian leaves the end of the sentence hanging not wanting to mention what happened.

"Thank you for that but I am kind of at a block. I keep drawing the same things over and over like there is nothing else I can see in my mind."

"Like what?" Ryan asks peering onto the page.

"Lots of butterflies, and I have never really been especially fond of butterflies but they seem special to me now."

"Maybe you just like the colors and how free they are since you are stuck in here," Jillian offers.

"Maybe, but then there is this old truck too."

"Do you know someone with a truck like that? It is a nice truck from what you are drawing," Ryan asks.

Nicole knows her drawing is still shaky and some of the lines cross and that they are just being nice complimenting her work that looks like a second grader did it. However, you can tell what it is and the style of truck is pretty cool like at a car show or something.

"No. I just keep seeing it in my head."

"Well, hey it's a nice truck," Jillian offers and Ryan excuses himself.

Outside of the room Ryan dials Agent Carr on his cell phone from the business card that she gave him.

He tells her that it is probably nothing but he needs to talk to her about something with Nicole. Agent Carr is happy to help Nicole in any way she can and asks him to continue.

"Well, I know nothing about the human brain or the psyche or anything but Nicole's been drawing and she keeps drawing this truck over and over and she does not know why. She says she doesn't know anyone with one like it or anything and I thought maybe it could be something from when she was missing."

"You know, it may or may not be. I am glad you called though I will make my way over there to check on her and see if I can tell anything from the pictures or from Nicole."

"I appreciate that, I don't want to upset her and she does not know I am calling."

"Don't worry, it will just be a normal visit from me, I know you are trying to help."

"One question though …"

"Yes …"

"You know what happened to her. I don't know very much and well, would it be better for her never to remember?"

"I honestly don't know. Part of me says yes because she would never have that pain or fear but part of me also feels that without facing it you never really get away from it. She has physical reminders that she will have her entire life even if she never remembers."

"Thank you Agent Carr."

"Thank you Ryan."

Ryan returns into the room and Nicole and Jillian are giggling giving the impression that they are talking about him. He takes that as his cue to say something cute and all three continue to joke and talk without discussing the drawings anymore. An hour passes and Agent Carr arrives in perfect timing as Ryan and Jillian are leaving. Agent Carr enters the room asking how Nicole is doing.

"Ok, I'm kinda glad you are here."

"Really, why is that?"

"Because my parents went to eat and such and I hate sitting here by myself I get so bored and the TV sucks in here," Nicole says with a laugh.

"Glad I can help. How are the hands doing? Are you listening to the doctors and limiting their use?"

"Trying to … sometimes I get drawing and lose track of time."

"How's the drawing coming?"

"It's getting better but still sucks."

"Can I see some?" Carr asks unsure of what to try next if she says no.

"Sure, I guess. But remember they suck."

"I am sure they are not that bad," Carr says as Nicole pushes the book over with the top of her hand.

Agent Carr opens the pages and starts looking through them without saying a word. There must be at least ten drawings of this truck in the last few days even with Nicole's broken hands. Carr thinks that Ryan may have been right and this may be a memory trying to come out of Nicole's head. Once she is done she sets the book down and turns towards Nicole who is looking at her with a longing look for approval.

"I think they are great and getting better each day."

"Ok, no sugar coating, just honesty."

"Honestly, they are rough but you can tell what they are and that you have a good ability for putting what you see down on paper."

"That's still a little sugarcoated but I'll take it."

"Good, cause that is all I am giving. You must like butterflies," Agent Carr decides not to jump right into the truck.

"I guess it's like I keep seeing them flying around in my head like they want me to draw them so they can be free … ok that sounded corny."

"No, I like butterflies. What about the truck? That must be your favorite kind of car or something?"

"No, I am not a big car person. It also is in my head like I need to draw it to get it out."

"Nicole, can I be brutally honest with you?"

"Yes, I expect you to."

"Ok, I wonder if that truck was one you saw when you were taken. I wonder if that was the car that took you. I know you can't remember but sometimes our minds do strange things and this may be your minds way of telling you something."

"Ok, so let me be honest."

"Ok," Agent Carr is a little nervous that Nicole may just throw her out and not talk to her.

"I have been having these dreams. Well … pieces of dreams really and that truck is in them with bright headlights coming right at me. I don't know what it means but in my dream I feel terrified of this truck."

"Thank you for telling me I know it can't be easy sharing things like this."

"Well, I can't really tell anyone because then they will freak out and treat me differently when I am just starting to feel a little like normal. I mean I am never going to be normal again but at least people around don't seem to be treating me as much like a broken doll or something."

"I understand what you mean. Tell me, if I bring in some pictures of trucks to you like the one you are drawing do you think you could pick it out?"

"Maybe. If I could only draw normal I could give you such a better picture."

"That's ok. I am going to go print up some pictures and I will be back shortly is that ok?"

"Yes, but if my parents are back …"

"I will take care of it."

Agent Carr is on her cell phone with Agent Fisher before she leaves the building telling him of her plans to bring the pictures back to Nicole and that she thinks it is the lead that they are looking for. Agent Fisher wants her to report back as soon as Nicole picks out a truck and he will start looking for it. When Agent Carr returns with the pictures the parents are there so she politely asks if she can have some alone time with Nicole and that she will come get them as soon as they are done. The parents having become comfortable with Agent Carr quickly agree and leave the room.

"So, here they are, take your time and let me know if any of them are close."

Nicole lays the pictures across her lap on the bed using the back of her hands to move them around. She looks at each for a few minutes saying nothing. Finally she shifts her entire body to the far side of the group of pictures and looks up at Agent Carr. Carr knows what she is going to say before she says it.

"This one has the same headlights and shape but wrong color."

"What color do you see in your head?"

"It is light, like gray or white or something," Nicole says with tears running down her face.

"Nicole, is there something else that you remember?"

"No. I don't want to remember. That is one feeling I am sure of … I am afraid to remember anything."

"That's ok. You have done great. I will pass this back to my team and we will start looking for him."

"You will let me know right, keep me posted?"

"Of course, I will."

Agent Carr heads to the police station where the team

is waiting for her. They have set up numerous televisions in the conference rooms with VCR's ready to review every piece of surveillance tape that Agent Fisher could think to grab. Every tape from the police station parking lot to the hospital security tapes, inside and out. Unfortunately, the housing development where the victim was found did not have any video surveillance. Agent Carr appears and scotch tapes the picture to a white board in the conference room the team has been using.

"Burke you take the hospital parking lot, Vickers you take inside the hospital, Dalton you take the police station parking lot. Carr I want you reviewing all the statements we took when the victim first went missing to see if anyone mentioned seeing a truck around. Keep me posted to anything you can find."

"Yes sir, getting started," Agent Dalton answers for the group.

The team continued to work through all the information they had in front of them looking for a lead. They did not take breaks and stopped only seconds to grab the food that was delivered for them to eat. At the end of the day they seem to have nothing. They continued to work throughout the night with no idea that the killer was already working on his next victim.

CHAPTER EIGHTEEN
Britney

———— ◊ ————

The police department in the town that Seamus has chosen has finally responded to the parents and taken the report of their daughter's disappearance as a serious missing persons case. They still have not notified the FBI team as they have not assumed that the bulletin released by them would have any correlation to the new missing persons report. The officers are still in debate about the accuracy of the missing persons report.

"You know this is probably one of the cheerleader pranks they have been told to stop doing, like the one where they kidnap the new cheerleaders in the middle of the night and take them to breakfast in their pajamas and then hold a practice on the field where the sprinklers always turn on when the new girls are practicing in their pj's."

"Yeah, but they usually notify the parents in some way first."

"Since they got into trouble for it now they may be keeping it a secret."

"Or something may have happened to this girl since it has been a couple days now I think we need to look into it in a serious way."

"Fine, I will post the bulletin and head to the school and ask some questions."

"Alright and I will talk to all the local convenience stores and such and make sure they post the bulletin for everyone to see."

"Sounds like a plan."

In the meantime, Seamus is working on his next phase of punishment. He likes antagonizing the girl and tightening the ropes every now and then so that she has trouble breathing. She continues to try to battle with him and that only excites him more, it proves that she does not respect men as she should and that she thinks that she can do whatever she wants. He is happy to prove her wrong.

"You are not looking so pretty anymore now are you," Seamus smiles down at her intending the comment as a put down and not a question.

She glares at him finding it hard to speak but continuing to kick her feet as he tightens belts around her legs forcing the swollen parts to swell outside the belts. Seamus learned with the prostitute that if he applied more pressure it caused more discoloration, bruising. He liked being able to see on the outside what was happening inside the girls body. He knew that her body was probably starting to shut down since he has been adding double the salt. He was also spraying her with water more often since it was not getting quite as cold at night as before. He looks into her face smiling and she tries to spit at him.

"You are a tough cookie, too bad you could not be a good girl." She looks up at him a little confused.

"Oh, now you're interested are you? You should have been listening before. I was trying to explain to you how I am saving you but you just kept fighting with me. It makes it hard to be a hero when the world doesn't recognize you yet, but they will. They will see that I taught you and saved all those people that you were going to hurt. I was watching you when you turned those boys away and laughed about it. If you were good you would not do that, you think you are better than them, better than me. I am showing you though aren't I, that you are not any better than anyone else, especially not me."

Britney closes her eyes hoping that if he thinks that she has went to sleep that he will shut up. She wonders where everyone is and why they have not come for her yet and why this crazy guy chose her. That was the biggest question in her mind, why, why her? Her legs were going numb but they still stung, she has stopped shivering and began not to feel anymore. Her mind seems to be slipping as she feels more and more tired and yet a part of her no matter how much she fights hopes that it will just be over soon. The pain started out unbearable and every time he tightened the rope around her stomach she thought she would stop breathing but she didn't. The pain was tolerable now and that worried her, either the pain was subsiding or she was no longer able to feel it. She had a feeling that it was the latter and knew that meant that she was losing. She did not want to stop fighting but she was so tired and she knew she could not take much more. As this thought crossed her mind she felt the first blow.

"I find that giving a good whipping to any animal is a good way to teach it. When an animal does something wrong you whip it and it does not do it again. People, especially people like you, they are basically just animals."

Seamus continues to use a belt and strike across Britney's body from her chest to her thighs watching the immediate welts and bruises that rise up on her skin. He watches and slows down as her skin turns the colors he wants to see then he sits back down across from her and enjoys a meal watching her wince in her sleep. He thinks to himself how sad it is that he had to start using more violent means of punishment. He knows though if he doesn't they will never learn. He thought that when he started making examples that some of them would stop or at least think but they did not and he is out numbered so he has to make a bigger statement and make it faster.

The police are distributing the flyers with Britney's picture as a missing person but so far no one can recall seeing her or anything out of the normal. The officer at the school has talked to all of the cheerleaders and they all say the same thing that there was no prank administered on Britney and that they don't know what happened. They admit to being in a fight with her over some gossip but say it was nothing and they are devastated that she is missing. The principal of the school confirmed that she is a good student and is sure that something must have happened to her.

Back at the police station the parents are talking to the police sergeant and asking to make a public plea for their daughter's safety. The sergeant agrees and offers to set up a media conference for them, he makes a few calls and then tells them that the soonest he could get some news crews out for a formal interview was the next day at noon. They were angered at having to wait but with no other recourse, agreed.

The next day at noon they held the conference that was scheduled and made a plea to whomever out there could help them in any way to please notify the police station and help them bring their daughter home. They offered a reward and asked for everyone in the community to help them find their daughter. The police sergeant spoke when they finished and answered some questions from the press. The conference was over in a matter of 20 minutes and the parents were left with little hope that it did any good at all.

The FBI team that remained in the dark about the new abduction was working in the conference room when one of the officers at that station barged in telling them to turn on the TV. They did and saw the end of the news conference. Agent Fisher was infuriated and instantly got onto the phone asking why they were not notified. Once he hung up he addressed his team.

"Well, the idiots over there felt that this girl that went missing was perhaps a prank that apparently the high school in the area is known for. The girl has already been missing for a few days and I told the sergeant that we will be there in the morning. Until then, Kid I need you to get on that computer of yours and map out the area. Find the most likely spots that she may be and call and give it to the department over there. Dalton start loading up and Vickers you need to help him. Agent Carr you need to go over to the hospital and inform the last victim that we are heading out of town and how to contact us if necessary."

The team split up to complete the orders dictated to them by Agent Fisher. They worked as fast as possible and it was not long before Agent Burke was on the phone with the police department telling them where to look for the missing girl. They said they would start looking right away. The team continued to pack up and was soon on their way to the new town and the new search hoping they were not coming in too late.

"There is a possibility that after losing the last victim that he may have escalated," Agent Carr starts the discussion as they travel.

"Escalated how?" Dalton asks.

"Well, last time it took too long for her to die on her own, he has to know since she was found that we will know where to look and he will have to speed up the process somehow with the next victim."

"You are assuming that he is that smart … how do we know that he won't just stay in the same routine that he already has?" Vickers asks.

"Well we don't know. I do presume him to have some intelligence since he manages to leave not a single trace of himself anywhere near his victims. The broken mind also tends to have a normal progression. If he has always been borderline as we suspect then once the event that broke him surfaced it started that progression. He went from in control to hunting young girls."

"And you think that the next stage for him would be to kill them himself instead of waiting for them to die?" Agent Fisher asks.

"Maybe, or to do something to speed up the death."

"Well, then it sounds like we are already out of time based on the timeline of the last victim," Dalton admits stating what they all were thinking..

" Maybe," Agent Fisher and Agent Carr say at the

same time. The rest of the trip is silent. They travel through the night and go straight to the police station.

"Good morning, sergeant can you please brief us as fast as possible on the victim?" Agent Fisher gets right to the point.

"Britney Shryder, 17 years old, senior at the local high school. She is a cheerleader and after going out with the team went home on her own, that is when she was last seen. Her car arrived at home, her parents found her keys on the lawn but she never made it into the house."

"Thank you. Have you been searching the areas that my team gave you?"

"Yes, we have it mapped out over here and each green area needs searched and each red area has been searched and found nothing," The sergeant leads the team to a large portable chalk board that has a large map of the city thumb tacked to it.

"Great, how many teams do you have searching?"

"I have five teams out now and have been calling in everyone I have since I spoke to you last night."

"Alright, then we will head out and help search," Agent fisher turns to his team and nods at them to get on their way.

The team splits up to search as they had before when they found Nicole. They were at the first site to search in less than 30 minutes and began searching with the hope that they would find the victim and be able to save her just as they did with Nicole. More over they all kept thinking that they really wanted to catch the killer more than anything. They want to stop this from happening again.

Seamus is cleaning up as the teams are out searching. He is calm and collected, he pours bleach over the entire area and then over the body limp on the floor in front of him. His plan to add in more punishment worked and he was able to speed up the process. This is good to him since that means he can punish more people this way. She died this morning a faster, untidy death but still satisfying to him. The fresh kill left him hungry for the next one. He would have to move on but he would never again wait so long in between. He only felt alive when they were dying. He already missed that feeling and wanted to feel alive again. He continued cleaning and started to hum. He was almost done. He packed everything up and headed to his truck cleaning any trace of himself along the way. He really liked that one, he thought to himself, she made it a little harder to teach but in the end he was able to complete the lesson.

Fisher's team got the phone call shortly after Seamus had driven away. One of the police teams found the victim. The victim was dead. Fisher instructed the team to the site where the body was found, he wanted to be sure that no one contaminated the scene. Agent Carr fought off tears knowing that she may be getting too close to the case. She could not believe that this guy got away again. She went to the vehicle the police station had given her for the search. After sitting down she dropped her head against the steering wheel, she felt hopeless. Agent Dalton climbed in next to her and said nothing at first.

"We will get him, we will," Dalton offers.

"After how many more?" Carr responds.

"You know how it is …"

"I know I just feel like we failed this time and I don't like failing." As Agent Carr is finishing this statement her phone begins to ring.

"Agent Carr."

"Hello, its Nicole."

"Hi Nicole," Agent Carr's voice falls low.

"I know you are busy but my friends, they saw the truck."

"What?" Agent Carr sits up straight.

"They saw the truck they think and the guy that drove it."

"Are they sure?"

"Yes, they say he was at the search and the hospital. They say he said his name was Nick."

"Does that sound familiar to you?"

"No. I have been having more dreams but I am not sure what any of them mean."

"Alright. Well let me talk to Agent Fisher and I will be on my way back to you."

"You are already done there? Did you find the girl?" There is some hesitation in Nicole's voice.

"Yes, we found her," Agent Carr really does not want

to share the news so she leaves it hanging in the air hoping that Nicole will take it as a good yes.

"And …"

"We were too late."

"Oh." Agent Carr can tell that Nicole is fighting off tears.

"I will see you tomorrow."

They hang up and Agent Carr calls Agent Fisher who is excited at having learned some information since he too was beginning to feel beat. Agent Fisher decides to leave Agent's Dalton and Vickers to help with the new victim and he heads back with Agent's Carr and Burke. They head out right away back to the police station they had only left the day before hoping that the information the friends provide will be enough to figure out who the killer is and hopefully enough to catch him before he kills again.

CHAPTER NINETEEN
New Information

———— ◊ ————

Agents Carr and Fisher arrive at the hospital to talk to Nicole in the morning. Nicole offers her apologies for the girl they were unable to save. Agent Carr asks for the details of the new information provided by the friends and Nicole picks up the phone to call them in to see the agents. In the meantime Nicole decides to share her interesting but frightening dreams.

"It does not make much sense to me but I keep dreaming that I am like drowning but not in a pool or anything just that there is water and I can't breathe. Probably nothing but," Nicole starts.

"We believe that the man who had you had been covering you in water to keep you cold," Agent Carr thinks that maybe by explaining possibilities that Nicole will feel more comfortable disclosing her dreams.

"Splashing water …"

"Ok."

"Also, I keep feeling like I am too far away from everyone … like no one can get to me or see or hear me and all I taste is salt."

"Well, the man we know uses salt we think to speed up the freezing of the water."

"Other than that I don't think I am much help, but my friends they seem to think they know who it is."

"Well, let's hope that they do and that they can help," Agent Fisher adds.

It is only a short time later that Jillian and Ryan enter the room. Jillian apologizes to the agents for not realizing before and informs them of all the people that she knows spoke to him. She has already called the other friends and they should be on their way.

"Well, what can you tell us?" Agent Carr asks eager for information.

"Well, there is this guy that we ran into at the store and the girls thought he was cute. Then when we went to the police station for the search for Nicole he was there too. The girls started talking to him, he said his name was Nick and his last name started with an S I think. He said he was there to help because he had a sister that went missing when he was little and people helped him. Then when Nicole came to the hospital he was here too.

One of the first days we arrived in the parking lot and he approached us asking how Nicole was doing. That was when we saw his truck he was parked in the lot out front," Jillian is talking so fast it is hard to keep up.

"He said he lived here but worked from home some internet company or something. He was in his twenty's or maybe even thirty. He has a pretty normal build not too tall maybe a little taller than me. Brown hair and that is all I can remember," Ryan adds.

"So everyone was around him the whole time?" Nicole looks scared as she says this.

"It is not that uncommon that people like this guy like to interject themselves into the investigation surrounding their crimes," Agent Carr offers to Nicole.

"Do you think that if we showed you surveillance tapes of the hospital here you could point out to us who he is?" Agent Fisher asks Jillian and Nicole.

"Definitely," Ryan responds before Jillian can say anything.

"Why don't you two come with me back to the station to review some tape and Agent Carr will stay here with Nicole," Agent Fisher is escorting them out of the room before he finishes the statement.

"Well, how are you?" Agent Carr asks Nicole once everyone else is gone.

"A little creeped out. This guy that did all this to me was around my friends and family. Not to mention I feel angry because I can't do anything about it."

"But you are helping ... if you had not drawn the picture of the truck to begin with no one would have put the two together and we would have no leads right now."

"Yeah, but I feel like I know more but I can't like access it or something. I just feel helpless."

"Well, how is your treatment going have you started any physical therapy or anything?"

"Yes, but only little bits they really don't want me going full force into rehabilitation until I am at least rested for six weeks from when I got here."

"Well that's not too long from now and I am sure once you are more mobile and getting ready to get out of here and go home you won't feel so helpless."

"I hope your right."

Back at the station Adria, Sarah, and Justin have all arrived to help Jillian and Ryan with all the tapes they have to look through. Jillian called them on the way to the station to tell them to meet there instead of the hospital. They all started reviewing tapes on different monitors with the help of Agent Burke and Agent Fisher. It was not too long before Justin found Seamus on the hospital footage.

"Hey, that's him right there. Stop the tape," Justin is pointing at the monitor.

"Ok, which one?" Agent Burke has the tape paused.

"Right there, that is him, he said he was there for a

physical with his doctor and saw us waiting… we told him that Nicole had amnesia."

"That may have saved Nicole's life. He must have moved on once he knew she could not identify him," Agent Fisher responds.

"I can zoom it in and get a picture of his face and run it through our software to make it clear," Agent Burke is already working on doing this.

"That's the truck," Adria is now pointing at another screen.

"Ok, can you get a license plate number Burke?" Agent Fisher asks.

"Hold on, I will be right there."

"Ok. You all have been so helpful. Is there anything else you can think of to help us locate this guy?" Agent Fisher is asking the whole group.

"Maybe if he used a credit card when he was seen at the store?" Ryan asks.

"Maybe, I doubt it but let's check. Give me the date and time and I will send an officer out to check on it," Agent Fisher responds.

"Sir, I can't get a license plate number but I can get a general picture of the truck," Agent Burke offers.

"Ok, sounds good. Run the picture of the guy through the system and see if you can get a hit."

"Will do, it will take a while."

Agent Burke finishes the software program to complete the picture of the killer and begins the program to compare it to all the records in the FBI database. The database includes every state and every counties records of arrest. All that was left now was to hope he had been arrested for something before. He waited watching the system as Agent Fisher escorted everyone out.

Once Agent Fisher returned he asked for Burke to take the pictures he had and to electronically send them out to all the police stations in the neighboring states as a top priority suspect. He hoped that if they did not get a hit in the system that at least they could start making the killer feel a little closed in when he sees his own picture on a wanted sign. He instructed Burke to be sure that all stations distributed the pictures to convenience stores and motels in the areas.

Jillian and Ryan headed back to the hospital to give Nicole the good news that they found the guy on the tapes. They arrived and Agent Carr headed back to the station. Jillian was excited to tell her friend that they were able to help and she started right away.

"We found him and now they are going to be able to catch him."

"Thank you for all of your help, both of you," Nicole says.

"Happy to help, anything to catch the monster that did this to you," Ryan responds.

"Thank you, I hope they are able to get him. Knowing he was so close to everyone and no one knew scares me."

"Honestly when I first realized the truck and this guy

went together I thanked god that Adria and Sarah did not go off with him. Not to say that ... shit ... I say everything wrong."

"No, I am glad too," Nicole says with a week smile.

"I am just glad that you are so strong and here with us again," Jillian smiles back.

"I am just glad that you are so beautiful and I am the only guy in here with you," Ryan says raising his eyebrow.

They all laugh and change the subject, it is not full closure of the scary issue that haunts Nicole's mind but it is a nice start. She hopes in her mind that someday soon Agent Carr will be able to walk into her room and inform her that they have him and that he is going away forever.

CHAPTER TWENTY
Getting Close

———— ◊ ————

Agent Burke sat staring at the computer as it ran every face stored in the system until late into the night. It had been running for hours nonstop and nothing yet. Burke was starting to think they were going to have no luck. Sometime in the middle of the night the computer stopped running through faces and stopped on one picture, a match. Agent Burke jumped out of his chair and hollered for Agent Fisher to come into the conference room. Agent Fisher was sleeping on the couch in the front of the station and jumped at the sudden noise of Agent Burkes yelling. He hurried into the conference room to see what was found.

"We got him, right here," Burke starts.

"Who is he?" Fisher asks.

"His name is Seamus Barack he was booked on fraud charges 6 years ago for cashing his mothers disability and social security checks for a year after she died."

"What is the most current residence we have?"

"The last known residence looks to be his mother's six years ago."

"Well, keep digging ... I want to know everything possible about this guy in the next hour and we will hold a press conference and see if we can not flush him out."

"You got it."

Agent Fisher calls his team and lets them know what they have found out. He knows that even though they know who the killer is now, they still cannot catch him without help. It does make Fisher feel closer to catching this guy simply by knowing who he is and he will make sure everyone knows who he is and hopefully they will find him before he finds his next victim. Agent Carr returns to the police department shortly after Fisher's phone call to her.

"So, what do we have, Fish?"

"Well, we know who he is and we are going to add him to the most wanted list," Agent Burke responds as though it is some small victory for them.

"Alright, we need to do more though."

"We are having a press conference and passing the information on to every department across the country. The police department here has offered to set up extra phone lines and get volunteers to man the lines," Agent Fisher explains.

"So we are going to count on tips to find him?" Agent Carr seems displeased with this idea.

"Well, we need the eyes of the people to find him unless he takes a new victim and I would like to catch him before he can take the next one."

"I agree. I just have to believe that there must be some way to track him, talking to people who knew him or figuring out why he does what he does. Tracking financials or something, did you put out an APB on his truck?"

"Description of the truck yes, the actual truck no. Apparently the Kid searched and he has no vehicle actually registered to his name or his mothers."

"What about any other relative? Can't we run a check on everyone in the area with that type of truck or with the same last name?"

"We will, I know you want this guy and so do I but there is only so much we can do in so much time…" Agent Fisher is trying to be understanding of Agent Carr's attachment to the victims in this case but is becoming a little frustrated with defending his decisions that he should not be defending.

"Fish, I know you want this guy too … we all do. I just want to be doing something not just waiting," Agent Carr realizes she is pushing too much and starts backing down a little.

"Alright then get a list from the Kid and start knocking on doors. See what you can find out about this guy from those people that knew him."

"Alright, thanks. I will keep you informed every step of the way."

"Sounds good," Fisher says while nodding his head towards the door telling her to be on her way.

Agent Carr gets a list of information from Agent Burke and heads out onto the road deciding to start with the property that the mother owned. Agent Fisher is meanwhile getting ready for the press conference and the rest of his team is heading back to his location. The press arrives a little early and seems restless. Agent Fisher is introduced by the police sergeant and begins telling the press and all the viewers the information obtained about Seamus.

"We now know who we are searching for and hope that with the new information we can prevent him from taking a new victim and be able to track his location based on everyone's attention and help. We know the type of vehicle that he drives and hope that will help girls that he targets spot him before he has the opportunity to attack. We will be posting the information online as well as distributing it to all the media outlets and police stations across the country. We want to also put a warning out there to parents so far the targets of these attacks have been young females, teenagers. They have usually been picked up at night so we caution against late activities or any activities that require being out alone. Now, that said that does not mean that he will only target females or younger people. We want everyone to be aware that the type of person or type of attack can change at any time," Agent Fisher has not so much as ended his sentence and the press starts asking questions.

"You say attacks, but my sources say deaths ... is this a serial killer?"

"We do not give titles. Yes, there have been some deaths but not all of the attacks have ended in death," Fisher is confident as he says this thinking of Nicole, his only survivor.

"You say you know who this guy is, how do you know?"

"Evidence has assisted us in identifying him," Fisher says shortly.

"You said not all the attacks ended in death so you have a witness to identify him?"

"No, I said we identified him from evidence collected," Fisher wants to protect Nicole as much as possible.

"If you knew the type of persons that were being targeted why is this the first warning being given to us?"

"We could not release any information until we were sure of the connection and what or who we were looking for," Fisher hates questions like that.

"So how many deaths are we talking?"

"I will not disclose information that could potentially hurt the case against this guy," Fisher is done talking and already backing away from the podium.

The police sergeant wrapped up the conference and made sure that all the necessary information was given to the media. Agent Fisher returns to the conference room to see if Agent Burke has come across anything new. Agent Carr should be calling soon as well as Agents Dalton and Vickers will be arriving at the station any minute.

Agent Carr is getting close to Seamus' mothers house. It is a small house in a rundown neighborhood. Agent Carr has made some calls on her way over and found out that no one currently lives in the house so she starts by talking to neighbors none of whom remember or want to try to remember Seamus or the mother. She is feeling a little hopeless and decides to check the local schools to see if any member of administration can remember them or could supply a yearbook with him in it so that she may track down classmates if need be. She arrives at the high school and is introduced to the principal who seems to be in his early 70's or so giving her hope that he would have been around when Seamus attended school and also a little concern that with his older age he may be having trouble with his memory already.

"It is nice to meet you. I need your help with an old student who would have attended here more than 10 years ago."

"Alright, let me sit down," the principal gets comfortable in his chair and turns his gaze back to Agent Carr to signify that he is ready.

"The students name is Seamus Barack. I have a

picture of him," Agent Carr hands the mug shot that Burke printed for her to the principal.

"He looks familiar, the name is a little fuzzy. Let me ask my assistant she has been here for twenty years but has a much better memory than I do," he calls the assistant into his office.

"Yes, what can I do for you?" The assistant asks.

"Do you remember this name or person …" the principal hands her the photo.

"Yes, he was here a long time ago. I remember he kept getting in trouble in his early years here and then he met a girl and they were inseparable."

"Do you remember the girl's name?" Agent Carr asks hopefully.

"Of course, sweet little thing, Cindy it was. She worked in the office here with me taking attendance calls and running slips to the classrooms for me. He was always in here visiting with her in the beginning of class and then back at the end of the period to walk her to the next."

"What kind of trouble did he get into before the girlfriend?"

"Oh, little stuff like firecrackers in the bathroom, smoking on the football field at lunch that kind of stuff."

"Oh, yes I remember him he used to be sent to me all the time for skipping classes," the principals memory seems to be jarred open by the assistant.

"Can I get whatever information you have on the girl?"

"Sure, thanks to computers now I can print it up in just a minute," the assistant runs out of the room only to return a few minutes later with a few printed pages.

"Thank you, you two have been most helpful."

As Agent Carr reaches her car she pulls out her cell phone and calls in to Agent Fisher giving him an update and asking for Agent Burke. She gives Burke all the information that she has on the girl and he tells her he will call her back shortly. It is about 15 minutes before her phone rings and Burke gives her the information she is looking for. She starts the car and begins to drive, the girl in question had only moved a few cities over and Agent Carr could be on her doorstep in just a couple hours.

As the team is getting closer to catching Seamus he is busy planning his next move. He saw part of the news conference on T.V. while eating at a diner off the highway. He was unsure of what information about himself was really out there since he only saw the end of the news broadcast so he decides to lay low. He checks into a small motel off the highway where the owner never even looked up from his newspaper as he checked him in. He went to his room and turned the TV on waiting for a new update that would tell him what they knew about him. He wondered if he should be more worried but deep down he felt that there was a greater force out there that wanted him to continue his work and would not let them catch him before all his work was done.

He sat on the edge of the bed watching the T.V. without moving for hours before he finally laid back and tried to close his eyes. He knew it would be no good that he would be unable to sleep without working on his tasks. He had a purpose and without fulfilling that purpose he could not be fulfilled in any way. He needs to find out what they know so he can adjust to continue his work. It was an hour more before he heard the news start with information about him. The first thing he decided must go was his truck since they had a picture of the type of truck plastered on the T.V.. He watched as they replayed parts of the news conference that talked about who he was. He thought to himself that they may know who he is now but that only means that he never needs to be caught for his work to be noticed. Everyone will already know who he is once they realize what a hero he truly is. He continued to think about things he could do to change his appearance a little like grow a mustache and beard and color his hair, that should be enough to keep the everyday people from recognizing him. He only needed to fool people for a few minutes like when he goes into a store for supplies or the few minutes it takes to pay for a motel room. He decides to go to the store and get the things he needs to change appearance and then he will dump the truck and buy an old used car cash. He would have to go to a junkyard or something somewhere he could get away with buying it and not worrying about a title.

Seamus is getting frustrated with all the things he has to do and that he must delay the next victim for a short period of time. He pulls himself up and releases a sigh, he hates that they have made it a little harder for him but at the same time is glad that he does not have to worry about it anymore. He will have to send a note to the Agent who was speaking on the news and thank him for making him famous. Fame is only a short step to his true calling, his ability to be a hero to all those people out there. He heads out writing the note in his mind that he will put on paper and send to Agent Fisher once he returns to his room.

Agent Carr has found the girls house that she is looking for and there is a car in the driveway. She steps out of her car and looks around, it is a suburban neighborhood. The neighborhood is clean and well kept and directly across the street from the house she is about to approach is a park with a playground. The woman she is about to meet must have children she thinks to herself. She walks to the door and rings the bell, a few moments later a tall woman appears at the door with a dishtowel in her hands busy drying them.

"Hello miss, I am Agent Rhonda Carr with the FBI are you Cynthia Thompson?"

"Yes, what can I do for you?" Cyndi is looking at Agent Carr with a worried look on her face.

"Can I come in?"

"Yes, come in," she opens the door and waves her arm inviting Agent Carr in.

Once they have sat down in the front room of the house on the couch Agent Carr notices the family photo on the side table and asks about the woman's children. Agent Carr wants to be sure that the children will not be hearing anything she will be telling the woman. The woman, Cyndi, acknowledges the pictures and says they are out at baseball practice and will not be home for at least another hour, they are alone.

"Ok, then I will get right to the point."

"Please …"

"According to your high school you used to date a Seamus Barack, correct?"

"Yes, that was ages ago, why?"

"Well, we are trying to locate Seamus and any information that you could give us could be helpful."

"What has he done?"

"We believe he has been killing young girls over the next couple of states," Agent Carr looks for a response on Cyndi's face as she says this but can not find one.

"The thing on the news this morning … I only saw the questions at the end I did not here that it was him."

"When was the last time you saw him?"

"Years ago, right after his mother died, he was a mess."

"What do you mean?"

"Well, I broke up with him almost two years before his mother died and he hated me for it. At first he would call me in the middle of the night and say that he was going to hurt himself or just die if we were not together again. I would try to talk to him but it was like he wasn't connecting things in his head right anymore. I did not see him for about nine months then I get this call from him that his mother died and him needing me to help with the arrangements. I felt bad for him, he did not have any friends it had been him and I for years and then when we broke up he just stayed in the house with his mother. So, I went over to help and the moment I showed up he acted like we had never been apart and never broke up it was a little creepy but I helped him with the arrangements and then left. He did not have a funeral service so I did not see him again. I spoke to him once more after that about six months after he called and said he had to see me that he couldn't eat or sleep and that it was time. I asked time for what and he said we were suppose to be together, well I did not know how to deal with him so I told him that I was with someone else and had been married the year before and was pregnant. He hung up on me and I did not hear from him again. I don't think anyone heard from him again. I feel like I am rambling, am I even helping?"

"Yes, you are helping. Anything I can learn to help me understand him will help me to find him. What was he like while you two were together?"

"Wonderful. He was kind and loving. He wanted to take care of me and make me happy. I think he would have done anything for me."

"Why did you leave him?"

"It was time to move on, I had met someone else and I felt that if I stayed with him I would always feel like I was in high school still. I wanted to grow up and have a family."

"And you did not see these things from him?"

"It was not that ... I think when it comes down to it I was swept off my feet by my husband that made me feel independent and loved. Seamus always made me feel like a child, someone for him to take care of, like a father more than a husband."

"What about Seamus' father?"

"Seamus' father left his mother when he was little he always thought it was because his mother had an affair. I could never tell who he was angrier at ... his mother for having the affair and making his dad leave or his father for not taking him with him."

"Did he ever regain contact with his father?"

"Not that I know of. He tried to find him after high school but he told me that his dad was a ghost that he would never find him."

"What do you think that meant?"

"I am not sure. Seamus would shut down if he did not like the topic of conversation and just wait until you changed the subject."

"Did he ever threaten you after you broke up?"

"No. He would beg and cry even but he never threatened me. He did however threaten to hurt my husband after I told him I was married and pregnant."

"You had been married for a year and did not tell him before?"

"No. I did not want to hurt him and he had changed I did not know what his reaction would be."

"So did he ever try to attack your husband?"

"No. I told my husband about it and he called and told the police who said if he did not physically do anything then they could not do anything. They said to call if he showed up here and he never did."

"Is there anything you can think of that may lead us to where he may go? For instance is there a particular food he likes to eat or anything he ever had to have?"

"I can't think of anything really … he had an allergy to strawberries so he does not eat much fruit but as for stuff he likes I don't know."

"Where did you two go out to when you were dating?"

"There was a café that shut down a couple years ago next to the movie theatres and we would go there and hang out and eat. He always ordered the grilled tuna sandwich."

"Alright. Well I have taken up enough of your time if you think of anything else would you please give me a call?" Agent Carr is already standing and handing her card to Cyndi.

"Oh, one more thing how old were you when you two broke up?"

"About 20 maybe 21."

"And when would you say was the turning point in your relationship?"

"About twenty I started looking for something more. The best time was right at the end and the summer after high school I thought I was so in love."

"Thanks again …"

Agent Carr left the house satisfied that she knew Seamus a little better and that she would be able to help in finding him. She called Agent Fisher and let him know that she was heading back to him with new information and wanted to have a meeting as soon as she returned to review the mental standings of the killer they are searching for. She drove fast and reached the station by nightfall, the team decided to man the phone lines for the night and hold the meeting in the morning.

CHAPTER TWENTY-ONE
Finding Seamus

——————— ◊ ———————

Agent Carr began the meeting by relaying the information she learned from the high school and then Cyndi to the team. Once she had relayed all the information she decided to break it down to them.

"I believe that he suffers from a borderline personality disorder he managed fine as long as he was able to keep control. When he started high school he started to feel out of control and started doing things to get into trouble like smoking, cutting class, being destructive. These were his ways of trying to establish control in a world dominated by adults telling him what to do. He began believing that women were bad at a young age when his father left his mother after she had an affair. His faith in women and relationships was restored when he met his first girlfriend Cynthia, although he was usually only comfortable as long as he could control her and the relationship. Eventually she wanted to be her own person and left him for someone else which was the first break in his mind. He believed in his mind they would get back together. He became like a recluse staying inside with his mother and never leaving the house. Then his mother died and left him alone. This was a bigger break in his mind and he reached out to fix it by trying to regain the relationship with Cynthia. At that time she told him she was married to another man and pregnant with her first child. This was the ultimate breaking point in his mind. He probably then began to see every woman as her until he could no longer take seeing her everywhere. He chooses his victims I think based on age and some likeness to her when he was happiest with her when they were finishing high school, teenagers. I think he may be taking these girls thinking that he can control them to keep them from leaving him like she did. In his mind he probably believes that if he keeps them from getting older he keeps them from leaving him."

"So he is attempting to change an outcome that already happened?" Dalton asks.

"Yes, in a sense he is."

"He thinks by killing them they can't leave him?" Burke says with a confused look on his face.

"Well, he either thinks he can control them to control his future or he thinks he can prevent them from doing the same thing to him like punishing them for what Cynthia did to him."

"So where do we go with this?" Agent Fisher asks.

"Well, arm the schools in the neighboring cities and states since we know he has to select the girls he is probably watching them and what better place to find teenage girls than at school. We also know that he will not go too long before taking another victim and he is traveling by truck so he can't get too far."

"I'll get on that right now," Vickers offers jumping up from his seat.

"We already sent his picture out to all the gas stations and convenience stores as well as a picture of the truck," Agent Burke tells Agent Carr.

"Alright. Send those same pictures to all the café's and diners and include in the description that he will be ordering a grilled tuna sandwich."

"What?" Agent Fisher looks bewildered.

"That is what he always ordered with Cyndi and he has an obsessive compulsive nature so he will continue to order the same thing."

"Ok." Agent Fisher still seemed a little confused.

While the team finds ways to get closer to finding Seamus he has already dyed his hair and disposed of the truck. He is on foot for the moment until he can find a new vehicle. He needs to eat and sleep and knows he must find someone soon. He walks by the high school and waits until the end of the day to see whom he should be teaching next. He finds a few good candidates and then heads to the closest used car lots asking about salvaged title cars and junkyards. The second lot he goes to sends him across town to a tow yard where they often have cars they sell out for cash. He goes there and finds the owner to be very helpful and for a little extra money he is willing to let the car go without the proper paperwork. Seamus drives away in an old damaged Toyota. He drives around town a few times investigating the different sites that he may use, this time he settles on an abandoned warehouse just on the brink of town. Other than maybe a drifter or two the place looks not to have been used in years. He is happy with his selection although he had to make it faster than usual. He returns to his room ready to proceed the next day with his plan.

The next day comes and Seamus is getting himself ready. He heads to the high school towards the end of the day and watches for the same girls from the day before. It is not long before one walks out with her nose in the air ignoring the guy walking behind her and talking. She is pretty and smiling but not paying attention to the people around her. He thinks she fits what he is looking for and waits for her to be alone. He does not have to wait long since she is in her car and on her way shortly. She stops at the local grocery store on the way home and he sees his opportunity. He waits for her return to her car and while she is putting the bag of her purchases in the car he grabs her, knocking her over the back of the head immediately so that she does not make a sound. Her body goes limp and he half carries and half drags it to his car quickly.

Seamus arrives at his chosen location with the girl and ties her up. He puts water and salt all over her and heads out. He has his routine and that routine includes getting his first good meal while she is still out. He will return and she should be awake and he will talk to her and eat his food. He always gets the same first meal, a grilled tuna fish sandwich so he heads into town to find a café where he can get a sandwich to go.

The FBI team has been working hard to get all the information they can out to every possible location that they can. Agent Carr has been on the phone reinforcing the severity of the situation and the need to catch this criminal before he takes another victim.

Agent Burke has continued to dig into all the details and evidence in order to build a case against Seamus. The rest of the team has been manning the phone lines and following up on leads. So far the majority of the calls have been dead ends.

"Fish, why is it that an open phone line brings out all the crazys?" Dalton asks sarcastically.

"Sift through the madness and find me a good lead," is Fishers short response.

"I just got off the phone with some lady who thinks this guy is her missing son, when I asked when he went missing she said 40 years ago … this is insane…" Vickers adds.

"We can go through a hundred bad calls if it gives one good one," Fisher glares at them to get back to the phones.

"Alright. Alright."

They continue to answer the phones and it is not too long before they get a good lead. Dalton answers the phone and at first he is not even really listening as a lady is almost whispering into the phone. Once she says she thinks the guy they are looking for is standing in her diner he perks up and begins asking questions.

"Mam, you say you think you saw him in your diner?"

"Not saw him. He is here now waiting for his food but he has different color hair. But the eyes look the same and he ordered a grilled tuna sandwich like it says on the bulletin the sheriff brought to us."

"And you are sure it is him?"

"Yeah, as sure as I can be but I do not see any truck like the one in the picture."

"Alright, give me the address I will have a police unit there in a few minutes." Dalton is snapping his fingers in the air and holding the phone with his shoulder as he is takes down the information on his notepad.

"His food is almost done …"

"Stall him if you can but only as long as you feel safe."

Fisher is standing over Dalton and as soon as he finishes writing Fisher snatches the piece of paper and flies to another phone to call the local police department in the area of the diner. He thinks to himself as he is giving instruction to the police officer on the phone that they may actually catch this guy. He looks over to where Agent Carr is sitting on the phone and waves at her to come over. He hangs up the phone and fills Agent Carr in.

"Your sandwich thing worked, he ordered a tuna sandwich and the lady recognized him. Or at least as far as we know she is right and it is him."

"I hope so, how far away is he?"

"Not too far passed the state line."

"So if we left now …" Agent Carr is ready to go.

"Let's go." Agent Fisher answers.

The team packs up and heads out as they are leaving they get a call from the police department sent to catch the killer. They missed him but they asked around the diner showing the pictures they were sent and everyone agreed it was definitely the guy. They knew this meant that he was still out there and probably already had his next victim, they needed to hurry.

Seamus however is oblivious to his close call at the diner. He received his sandwich and headed back to the building his victim was in. He arrives to her screaming and laughs knowing that no one can hear her. Her screams bounce off the cement walls from one area of the warehouse to another becoming quieter and quieter until they reach a door and sound like nothing more than a small bird. He enters the building and sits down across from her and begins to eat his sandwich watching her try to get out of the ropes. He enjoys his food while she yells at him. She is talking tough but he can tell in her eyes that she is scared. He thinks to himself about how he wishes this part could go on forever, the good company, good food, and good memories, but realizes that is not his purpose. His purpose is to prevent her from hurting people like him. He has to teach her a lesson even if it means that he will then have to go hungry for a while. His hunger is his guide to tell him when he needs to teach again. He can feel inside how important he is and knows he must continue on.

She is sill fussing and is trying now to spit at him but is coming nowhere close. He begins to talk to her and tell her how he is helping her and how he is protecting the world from her just as he had told Nicole. He is enjoying sharing his gift with someone and his ability to be a hero. She has stopped fighting him and now only looks at him with a confused look on her face. She closes her eyes waiting for him to go away. It takes some time but he does eventually leave after spraying her again with water promising to return soon and start the next lesson. She keeps her eyes closed realizing she is more scared than she has ever been in her life.

Agent Carr and Fisher are in one car on the way to the small town that called in the sighting of their killer. The rest of the team had to wait for relief on the phone lines but were following not far behind. Agent Carr was not happy that the police had missed Seamus at the diner but was hopeful since they now had at least had an idea of where Seamus was. She was also worried because she knew if he was having his sandwich then he found a replacement for Cynthia. She was rambling on about all of these feelings to Fisher as they drove along.

"It's transference. He believes that the girls that he takes are this old girlfriend. He is punishing them for her leaving," Fisher responds.

"Yes, but part of me thinks maybe there is something more to it."

"Like what."

"I am not sure but we have enough to find him and right now that is all that matters…saving the girl he has taken."

"Well at least we already have a model, we know where to search."

"Yeah, Burke sent that over to you already right so we can get started without waiting for them?"

"Yeah he already divided the areas and we will start right into looking as soon as we check in at the police station and they will just head straight into searching, it should put us at about the same point at the same time," Fisher kind of gives Carr a look that says "are you questioning me?"

"I am sorry," she references the look. "I know you will

have covered all areas I just don't want to lose another vic to this guy."

"I know and neither do I. I want to catch this guy you just need to remember that you are not the only one fighting to save this girl or find this guy before he can finish what he has started."

"I just want to be able to tell Nicole we got him and stop him from hurting anyone else. We are almost to the station."

They arrive at the station and begin to exchange the necessary information starting with the description of the areas to search and assigning search teams. The rest of Fisher's team has arrived and started searching sites calling in each clear as they clear it. The search teams receive assignments and each head out. Agent Carr and Fisher return to their own vehicle to begin searching the areas they are assigned.

CHAPTER TWENTY-TWO
Catching Seamus

———————— ◊ ————————

Agents Dalton, Vickers, and Burke were traveling from location to location checking the empty buildings in the area they were assigned. Burke pounded away on his computer while Vickers and Dalton argued over the next best place to look. Ultimately they waited for Burke to tell them which area to check next before they moved on despite what either of them argued. They are moving closer and closer to Seamus without knowing it.

Meanwhile Seamus is using a pair of scissors to remove the clothes from the victim's body letting them land like a wet blanket held down by her body. He continues to wet her body and add salt and is now forcing caffeine tablets into her mouth since she refuses to take the water he offers. He found that if he removes the clothes he can watch the skin on the body change colors to purples and blues and intensify his enjoyment. He also found that if he wants to increase swelling when he abuses the body he needs to be able to see the skin, the clothes protect too much. He also likes the reaction he gets when he begins to cut the clothes as they cringe, shaking and crying. They fear that he may take advantage of them but that is not part of the lesson. He is reliving the look on her face and not paying attention to his surroundings as a car is pulling into the warehouse area that he is in.

"This is the next closest location in the area. Let's check here," Burke is telling Dalton and Vickers.

"Alright, I will start at the left and you at the right," Dalton starts.

"And we will meet in the middle where the kid will be waiting for us and watching all exits," Vickers finishes.

"Sounds like a plan," Dalton has turned off the car and is already climbing out onto the gravel road in front of the abandoned warehouses.

They start to walk to the ends of the block unsure if the several buildings in front of them connect or if they are going to have to search each place entering and exiting in between. Agent Burke watches as they enter the buildings but is still working on his laptop on the back of the car. Agent Fisher and Carr are on the other side of town heading through their list of locations as quickly and efficiently as possible.

Seamus is getting tired and hungry so he is finishing

up with his victim and getting ready to head to the motel for a shower and sleep he will finally be able to enjoy. He packs up and cleans the area getting ready to leave. He is so wrapped up in his own thoughts that he does not hear the agents outside.

Vickers steps outside the second building and hears someone walking he draws his gun and searches in front of him trying to see where the noise is coming from thinking to himself that it may only be Dalton making noise. He is the first to spot the movement of someone coming out of the warehouse towards the middle of the grouping. He waits, walking slowly and trying not to make any noise wanting to get as close as possible without being seen. He creeps forward but Seamus hears the clatter of the laptop keys from Burke at the car and starts to run from the entrance of the warehouse.

"Dalton he's coming your way," Vickers yells hoping Dalton is close enough to grab the guy that he thinks is the killer they are looking for.

Agent Burke hears the commotion and sees Seamus with Vickers following. He knows that means that the victim is inside the building so he runs into the warehouse to find her. He does find her and calls it in to get her an ambulance and calls in back up for Dalton and Vickers. He tries to see if there is anything at the site where he found her. He looks for any evidence or clues that he should take note of before there are too many bodies in the way.

"You are going to be okay. Help is on the way. It's okay." Burke repeats over and over to the victim while placing his jacket over her body.

Outside Vickers is trying to catch up with Seamus but is not closing the distance. Dalton heard Vickers and heads straight for the door of the warehouse he was searching. He exits gun drawn at almost a sprint just behind Seamus, seeing him lights a fire inside him that both increases his speed and his anger. He is gaining on Seamus and as Seamus reaches his car Dalton lunges forward at him pinning him to the car and then forcing him to the ground to handcuff him. Vickers arrives seconds later and helps drag Seamus to his feet they start to walk him to the car, towards all the flashing lights. They are not saying a word to Seamus and Seamus is just walking head low keeping his mouth shut.

Returning to the car Burke is standing with a few police officers as he calls Agent Fisher to let them know where they are and find out what he wanted them to do next. Fisher is angry that the police may be contaminating the scene but is glad to hear that they not only found the victim but the killer. He tells Burke he will save the rest of his questions for once they arrive and tells him to send Vickers with the victim so he can be available to question her as soon as she is stable.

"Well, we got him and the girl is still alive," Fisher turns to Carr.

"Who is taking him in?"

"For the moment the local police are going to house him until we finish up the scene and obtain the statement from the victim. The sergeant has been given instruction to hold him without any contact until we arrive."

"Good, I would hate to have them screw up the interrogation."

"Yeah, so let's get busy. The less time they have to screw it up the better."

"How is the victim?"

"Unconscious is all the Kid said, we will find out more from Vickers once they get to the hospital and the doctors are with her."

"Alright."

"Prepare yourself though Rhonda, this time was different. He said the victim's clothes had been cut off, we have not seen that before from this killer."

"Something made him change we will have to wait to see how bad it is. We are almost there so let's see what we can find out," Agent Carr turns off the car and climbs out as Dalton walks up to the car.

"I have been circling every angle of the site and already had the car sent back to headquarters for the investigators to tear apart for evidence. I am finding more local officers trampling evidence than I am actually finding evidence."

"What do you mean? He must have left evidence here," Fisher is angry at the news Dalton is giving him.

"Not much of anything he apparently bleaches and

cleans before he leaves each time, the only new evidence is the rope, it is usually removed before we find the bodies. It is already bagged and sent on to evidence," Dalton answers shaking his head.

"You have got to be kidding me. Well you continue to try and control the scene and we will head back to interrogate. Good job today," Fisher says while reaching up and patting Dalton once on the back of his shoulder.

Dalton heads back into the warehouse and Agent Carr and Fisher head back to the police station to talk to Seamus. Upon arriving at the station Agent Carr practically jumps out of the car before even turning it off. They enter the room where Seamus sits and he looks up at the two of them with a blank look. Agent Carr knows that she is emotionally tied to this case so she waits and lets Agent Fisher go first.

"Well, it is nice to finally meet you Seamus," Fisher says sarcastically while trying to bait the killer into bragging.

"We have been following you for some time. I am Agent Fisher with the FBI."

"Is there anyone in there?" Carr asked with attitude since Seamus keeps staring blankly back at them with no answer. This last comment caused Seamus to smirk.

"Sorry, but I believe I need my attorney present to speak with you," Seamus says plainly.

"You have an attorney?" Carr responds snidely.

"Not yet, but I am sure once you announce that you

have me on the news they will be lining up to defend me. It will be a highly publicized case I am sure and lawyers always look for the limelight."

"So you plan on making this quite a public trial," Fisher muses.

"Well once you tell the world that you have a serial killer they will pay attention and once my attorney tells them you have no proof to hold me on then you will really have their attention."

"What makes you think we don't have proof?" Carr asked.

"I know. Now I will say nothing more until I see my lawyer."

"You are pretty cocky …"

"No, just smart."

Agents Fisher and Carr exit the interrogation room unhappy. Carr is shaking her head and has an angry expression on her face. Fisher is watching her wanting to make sure she is ok and not overly reacting to the brick wall they just encountered.

"I can't believe he really thinks …" Carr says letting the end of the sentence fall out into the open air.

"We need to find out where we really are based on evidence. He is right the sharks will be circling and there will be quite a media circus."

"I will get everyone together and find out what we have and what we need."

"We should transport him out and find out who is

prosecuting so that we have a head start to this case. I have a feeling we are going to need it because once he is out in the media we will have all kinds of new issues."

"Yeah, every person with a loved one missing is going to think he may have done it and begin calling in looking for information and such. It will be crazy."

"It will be very publicized so the jury pool will be small and the risk of exposure of evidence could really hurt us … we need to find out what the prosecution needs from us so that we are not out chasing this guy again."

"I will call you as soon as the meeting is set up and we are ready to talk details, Fish."

CHAPTER TWENTY-THREE
Prosecution

———————— ◊ ————————

I t is just over 24 hours later but the team is together with the prosecution and the suspected killer, Seamus has been moved. It has taken quite a miracle but the media has not yet found out that they have him custody. The meeting is about to start and the team and everyone else in the room seems quite anxious.

"Allow me to introduce my team and thank you all for coming on such short notice. We are holding this meeting under strict confidence and have less than 24 hours before we have to charge the suspect in custody and assign him an attorney. At that time all hell could break loose so we as a team need to be sure that we have this case locked and loaded before a trial begins," Agent Fisher begins the meeting and introduces each of the team and leaves Agent Carr to introduce everyone else present.

"With us today we have the federal prosecutor, his team, assistant, and his superior. Also here are a couple of the techs from the crime lab. We have provided you all with every report we have and now I will leave you in the hands of our prosecuting team."

"I am Federal Prosecutor Bill Rydell. I have spent the last 24 hours reviewing the arrest and every note I can find on the case. Agent Fisher has been keeping me up to speed throughout the case and now here we are attempting to prove what we know … that the man we have in custody is the same man that we have been following from state to state killing young girls. I have questions for the FBI team that has been tracking him but the lab technicians will first tell us what the evidence throughout the search has produced."

One of the technician's stands to speak and the other tech hangs her head. They look at each other briefly before the tech standing up begins to tell the group before him that he does not have the evidence that they are all hoping for.

"We have collected everything from each area that we know the killer acted in but we are coming up short on the evidence we need," the tech starts.

"What do you mean? How could we not have what we need? What about the killer's vehicle and supplies when we found him?" Agent Carr asks.

"Well, the car was clean and we have not found the truck yet. The car had no blood, no fingerprints other than his own, no sign that anyone was ever in the car."

"No strands of hair or anything in the carpet or trunk?" Rydell asks with a look of frustration on his face.

"We found slivers of rope but we have been unable to prove that they came from the rope used on the victims."

"How is that possible? The rope was still on the last victim when we found her," Vickers asks.

"The rope was but there is nothing distinctive to prove it is the same rope, only that it is the same type you can buy at any hardware store and that leaves doubt."

"Well, what about the rope itself or the victim's clothes?" Rydell asks hoping that the technician started with the bad news and he was only waiting to hear the good news.

"Unfortunately nothing."

"Nothing …?" Fish asks.

"Nothing, the rope was drenched in bleach, common household bleach and no clothing particles or fingerprints or anything that tied the suspect to the rope or the victim's clothes."

"What about the bottle of bleach itself? It had to be there at the location or in the car," Rydell's assistant offers letting the last part of the question fade into the open air so that the question seems more like a statement about the work done by the local police and the crime lab.

"There was nothing in the car to tie him to the scene no bleach, no rope, nothing to cut her clothes as they were. We searched the area around each location where the victim was found and could not locate any of the supplies we assume he used. There was nothing but water and bleach at every location."

"So what did he do with everything then?" Carr asks feeling a little disappointed.

"We think that he dumped it, hid it, or burned it. We found some ash near the sites that seem to point to him burning the evidence. We are unsure of what he may have done with the items he used at the latest site where we found him. There are a few items that we have found in the area that are still being processed but we can not be sure that any of them are actually his or that we can tie them to him or the scene. The only thing we found that we know is related is a pair of scissors that he must have used to cut her clothes because we found pieces of cloth in them that matches her clothes."

"Did you find fingerprints or anything to tie them to the suspect?" Rydell asks hoping for a yes.

"No, we found them in the gutter along the area that the suspect fled, they were covered in water, dirt, and other elements. We are processing a few other items like this on a rush."

"And we do not have anything from the previous scenes?" Fisher asks.

"We have the surveillance video that the truck and the suspect were identified in. How about the witnesses that identified him?" Rydell addresses Fisher's team.

"They are willing to testify but they are only witness to the suspect using the truck and the victim that identified the truck did it in a drawing from one of her dreams," Carr answers knowing how bad the explanation sounds.

"So what we actually have is him at the location of the final victim, him at the hospital and search party locations for the previous victim that survived and his behavior with his high school girlfriend?" Rydell seems to be getting mad.

"Let's play this out," one of Rydell's team offers up in assistance.

"Ok. He is at the location we picked him up where we find the latest victim," Rydell starts.

"He had no idea that the victim was there and had nothing to do with what was happening to her. He simply was in the wrong place at the wrong time."

"Then why did he run from the agents that apprehended him?"

"They were not in a marked car or uniforms he saw only men with guns out and he ran out of fear."

"Why did he change vehicles from the last time he was seen and why was he traveling?"

"His truck broke down so he got the next cheap car

he could he is traveling across the United States because he wanted to leave his home town once his mother died and he wants to see everything he can."

"So how is it that he just happened to be traveling along the same route as the killer?"

"Coincidence … unless you can prove otherwise."

"The girlfriend that broke his heart gives us examples of his unstable mind and psychologist say that he picked his victims based on her."

"Yeah, he had his heart broken and she felt he was weird but he never hurt her and if he wanted to hurt her he had access to do it and did not. She could also be the reason that he left town to travel to get his mind off of her and her family."

"Ok … and the search party and hospital where the previous victim was at?"

"He was staying in the area at the time and he wanted to help out when he heard the girl was missing. He was concerned and after she was found he went to the hospital for an actual doctor's appointment for himself since no one saw him anywhere near the victim's room there is nothing to connect him to her."

"So … does everyone here get the picture? We need more to keep this guy locked up. This guy will have the best lawyers out there because it will put that lawyer in the spotlight of a high profile case. We have to have all our T's crossed and I's dotted … there is no room for error. We have no weapon, no confession, just circumstantial evidence. We can charge him on that but I need more, get me the evidence I need or this guy will be back out on the street," Rydell stands and his team follows as they exit the room the techs following with there heads down.

"Any ideas of how to make the charge stick?" Fisher asks his team.

"What happened to the days where we caught the bad guys and handed them over it is not our job to make it stick or to prosecute the criminals. We catch them and they are suppose to finish the job," Dalton is frustrated and wants to vent.

"We do not want this guy back on the street it may be a little easier to find him next time but how many girls will have to die until we can collect enough evidence?" Carr responds angry that they are back to square one.

"Why don't we see if we can strengthen what we already have and let the locals and the lab work on new evidence?" Vickers asks.

"That is not a bad idea. Why don't we retrace the steps we have taken and talk to the locals and such? We may find new things or we may just be able to build a stronger case of what we do have," Fisher directs each of his team members to different tasks and they disperse feeling beaten wanting to accomplish the task of keeping this suspect behind bars.

CHAPTER TWENTY-FOUR
Media

———— ◊ ————

The team arrived in different cities with their assignments and it was no time at all before the media was pouring the information of the arrest all over the airways. The radio was reporting it and the television was covered with breaking news reels stating that the serial killer the FBI has been looking for was caught. They had only a small amount of information from which to start from but the publicity had already attracted a few large sharks who had made their way to meet with Seamus and offer their services free of charge.

Seamus sat at the small plastic table in a small room designed for this kind of meeting at the jail. He waited with a pleased look on his face as each lawyer paraded themselves in front of him wanting his approval, the job of defending him, and the publicity of what would be a high profile case. The first few seemed like a joke to Seamus and he almost laughed as he shook his head no and waved them away before they even began speaking. Then a small framed woman walked in, probably an outstanding attorney but a woman and Seamus was only angered by the thought that they understood him so little that they would send her in to him. The next attorney was a little too obnoxious and then finally the right man entered the little room. Seamus stayed in his seat and watched as the man pulled up a chair and offered his card.

"Why are you here?" Seamus asks shortly.

"You need an attorney and that is what I do," the attorney answers.

"Beyond that …"

"Let's be real … this is a high profile case that I can use to promote my career and you need the best. I believe I am the right person to represent you."

"Honest," Seamus mused. "Why you?"

"I understand you and can get you cleared of the charges. I want to help you share your story with the world and mostly I like to win, I don't like losing."

"What's your record in the courtroom?"

"I have lost only one case when I first began practicing law. I have not lost a single case since."

"Are you married?"

"No."

"Do you have children or a girlfriend?"

"No ... it is just me and my work."

"Alright. You are my attorney and at no cost."

"Alright, then lets get down to business, what do I need to know and what do you think they are basing your arrest on?"

"You jump right in, don't you? That is good. They can't be basing it on much other than my unfortunate luck of being in the wrong place at the wrong time."

"You mean where they arrested you at? Why were you in the area?"

"I was all over that town looking at old buildings and new architecture I have an interest in it. Sometimes think that I may have made a good architect if I would have gone thru some sort of schooling."

Seamus was lying through his teeth and although his new attorney may have suspected as much he showed no sign of caring if it was the truth or not. The relationship between the two was going to be a good one. They seemed to understand each other. They delved into the details of the case the district attorney may have as evidence against Seamus. There was one question that was eating at the back of Seamus' mind so he proceeded to ask it as soon as the subject arose.

"The girl they found; does she recall anything from her experience?"

"The girl who witnesses say saw you at the search party for and the hospital?"

"Yes, I felt bad for that community when I was passing through and thought I would help out and look for her with them. Then I went to see the doctor there and saw some of the same people from the search. I spoke with them and they said they were friends with the girl and that the girl had no memory."

"That is the same story now … she cannot remember anything from her kidnapping."

"That's too bad she could have told them it was not me," Seamus says with a smirk. In his mind he is thinking about how they knew to talk to the group of kids that are playing witness if she did not remember anything. He wonders if they are lying about the information that the girl has contributed or if he missed something else.

"Well, it sounds like they do not have anything substantial to charge you with and a circumstantial trial of this magnitude will create waves in the media and the courts."

"What do you mean?" Seamus asks knowing the answer, having counted on the answer.

"Well the media is going to attack the FBI for charging you without enough evidence. If they think you are the serial killer they have been looking for then they will attack the agency for not building a stronger case and if they think you may not be then they will attack them for holding an innocent man while the real killer goes on killing unwatched. The courts will not want to tie up time or space as well as they will not want to be seen in the public eye as allowing a man to be tried without evidence or wasting time while the real killer walks free."

"So you believe this case will be high profile …"

"Isn't that what you counted on by waiting on a lawyer to come to you and not the other way around?"

"Yes, I saw it on the news a few times and people may not really care about each other but everyone cares about kids."

"You are right. I will approach the federal prosecutor and see what I can find out."

"Thank you. I will see you soon," Seamus is happy with his decision and is correct in his thought process; the media is already dissecting the case for him.

Seamus' attorney leaves and he is returned to the general population at the jail. He goes straight to a chair to watch the news, the news about him. He knows that the public will recognize that he does not belong in the jail. He will be out soon and will be able to carry on with his lessons. He believes in the judicial system working for the criminal and allowing him to continue on free because of that little thing called reasonable doubt. He knows there will be at least one juror who will see things clearly, the way that he does and will not let him go to jail for doing the right thing.

The attorney on the other hand was also counting on that little thing called reasonable doubt. However, the attorney was counting on the media and assumed lack of evidence to furnish the doubt. The media will tear apart anything that the prosecution has to present. These days the higher profile the case the more likely the case will be too corrupted by exposure for anything other than an acquittal. The attorney also knows that every report will include his name and once he wins the case he will be able to charge a fortune to every high profile case that he takes on.

The media continued to profile the case discussing the importance of keeping killers like Seamus off the street while still using words like alleged and suspected. The media was making Seamus and his story famous. The attention had not gone unnoticed by the networks and major movie producers either. Seamus would have offers for a book shortly and not long after he would be offered a movie deal for his story. He knew he would beat the charges but then he needed to continue on his journey of helping and teaching. He thought to himself how much easier it would be to provide these lessons with the money that fame would bring to him. He would have everything he needed at his closest disposal and the money to get anything he didn't. He would be feared and favored as a serial killer in today's society. He would be able to tell his story and show the world what a hero he is. Once his story is out there will be others to continue his work maybe he will be able to just enjoy in there teachings. His stomach growls as he smiles at his own thoughts and his own plan. He still cannot eat, sleep, or enjoy anything without someone else going without he must get out soon so he does not become too weak.

CHAPTER TWENTY-FIVE
Nicole

———— ◊ ————

Agent Rhonda Carr arrived at the hospital to see Nicole, she wished she was only there to visit and give Nicole the good news that Seamus could never come back to hurt her but that was not the case. Agent Carr was there to find out what new information Nicole could remember and see what help she could be to the case. She walked into the room where Nicole was working with a physical therapist and quietly waited at the door until the therapist left.

"Hello Nicole, you seem to be healing and improving remarkably fast," Carr offers a compliment to Nicole in hopes of softening the discussion before it begins.

"Hey Rhonda how are you?"

"Ok, I wish I was here under better circumstances."

"I figured I would be seeing you soon … I have not watched any of the news but Jillian told me that you caught him," Nicole has a forced smile as she tells Carr that she was expecting her.

"I need to talk to you about what happened and see if there is anything that can help us," Carr says searching Nicole's face for any expression that will tell her what she is thinking.

"I actually was talking with Ryan about how the more time goes by the more I seem to remember but it is in such little pieces and usually in my dreams or my drawings. I am not sure how much that can help."

"What have you been remembering?"

"Small things like bits from the party that night and lights blinding me, I think they are headlights. Then there are things like salt … lots of salt. I can not eat anything with salt on it I start to feel sick. I remember cold and salt and when I dream I feel scared, alone, and it leaves me with a shiver that runs all through me," Nicole pauses her throat tightening up and tears building in the corners of her eyes.

"That is actually very helpful, is there anything else?" Carr feels like crying herself at having to ask these questions after everything Nicole has been through.

"Yes. I was drawing things and I started drawing pieces of his face as well as the truck. He talked to me but I can not remember what was said. I can't remember if he touched me or when my fingers … or … I want to remember more but ... it is ... I do not want to remember some of it," Nicole lets her voice fade and Agent Carr takes her hand and squeezes it slightly.

"I want to be able to tell you that we can put him away and you never have to worry again but that would be a lie. We need more to put him away, your friends they will testify right?"

"Yes I am sure they will, at least Ryan and Jillian will. I can too but I am not sure what all I can say ..."

"You can tell them how you are now, what you are going through because of what he did to you and then leave it to us to tie it all together," Carr starts but is interrupted by Nicole.

"I read something once or saw in a movie where they can hypnotize you to make you remember things you have forgotten or otherwise blocked out. Could they do that to me?"

"That is a very brave question but I have to say I would not suggest trying that method. Sometimes we mess with things we should not be messing with and if your brain has managed to block out memories that are harmful to you there is a reason for it. Those memories should stay blocked until the brain feels your consciousness is ready to deal with it. As for you I would strongly argue with any doctor willing to try it on you. You have amnesia caused by actual harm to your body it is a safety precaution that your body has where the brain removes memories before it allows other areas to completely shut down. I don't know how to stress how important it is that you not undergo any type of procedure or experiment that could traumatize your system in any way. It is better to have you healthy and healing than in a coma where you cannot help at all," Carr feels like she is rambling and Nicole is looking at her with a blank look so she stops talking and waits for some type of response from Nicole.

"I appreciate you caring about me so much but if he isn't locked up I will spend my whole life waiting for him to come back after me and I don't want to live like that."

"I understand but it takes most victims a long time to come to that realization and even longer to come up with enough courage to face it. Some never reach that point. I would hate for you to lose that courage or go backwards because you had to face things that your mind is not ready to."

"Alright, I will continue to record every little thing I remember," Nicole says a little confused and a little relieved that she would not have to face the things that scare her when she sleeps.

"You have been recording all of the things you remember?" This sparks some interest in Carr.

"Yeah, it is on the chair in the corner you can take it with you," Nicole uses her arm to gesture towards the chair.

Agent Carr picks up the notes and takes them with her. Nicole lays down to rest and dream again. Carr starts flipping through the notes in the elevator but everything in the notes is like a puzzle to Carr. The parts she did understand were in fragments and not complete. As Agent Carr walked to the car she realizes that they do not have enough to put Seamus away. In time Nicole may get enough of her memory back to properly identify Seamus and put him away but probably not before he is tried, acquitted, and double jeopardy has applied. She hopes that her teammates are having better luck than she is and calls Fisher to check on things.

"The latest victim has not done as well as Nicole did and is unable to talk at all at this point, she seems to need to learn to do everything again … like walk, talk, etc. Without Nicole I am afraid we have a really weak case but you can present what you have to Rydell and see what the prosecutors decide," Fisher directs Carr.

CHAPTER TWENTY-SIX
The Decision

———— ◊ ————

The team has assembled again with the prosecutor's office and techs from the crime lab to see what new evidence was found and what steps to take next. Everyone in the room looks sullen. Their expressions resemble the look your face gets when someone close to you has just died. No one really needs to hear it said aloud they all know they are facing an uphill battle with a slim chance of winning. They also know that if they let him go they may be unable to find him again or worse, he will kill again.

"I have reviewed everything that all of you have sent to me and I am open to any idea of how to keep this guy behind bars," Rydell is looking around the room at everyone waiting for a positive response.

"We are processing everything and anything we can

get our hands to try to make a connection that will stick. We don't know where else to look," One of the lab techs says with a defeated look on his face.

"I think all we really have is witnesses putting him at one and then catching at another scene, and then his past. Also if everything goes right we will have two psychological reviews from top accredited psychologist. Their findings, the witness statements, and the truck drawing produced by our surviving victim," Rydell states.

"Our surviving victim? I thought the most recent victim was in a coma but surviving?" Dalton questions.

"Well, about an hour ago I got the call that she had past," Rydell is finishing the sentence as Carr makes a small noise that sounds like a gasp and everyone turns to her.

"Sorry. I just have this horrible feeling in my gut."

"I think we all do," Fisher adds.

"Well. I think we rely on making the jurors see the horrible picture of someone out there torturing and killing children, especially beautiful young teenagers. We aim at a jury pool of parents and females the other side will want the opposite. We are going to have to play on people's fears," Rydell begins explaining the strategy.

"One problem … in today's society serial killers are not just feared but loved. He will be glamorized and his story will make some feel sad for him and really if he gets any type of attorney that knows what he is doing then they are going to play the fear card right back against us. They will play on people's fear of "what if". What if he is not the killer and we are exposing the only evidence we have? What if we stop looking after he is convicted and someone is still out there hunting young girls but in some way that we don't know it is the same guy? You know like the killer takes it as a sign to change his ways when we lock up this guy," Rydell's assistant is playing devils advocate.

"I have a suggestion to make perhaps we decide what charges to bring against him first then plan the case," Fisher seems annoyed.

"I think that is a good idea," before Rydell finishes Carr interrupts her.

"I believe that we should wait to charge for the attempt on Nicole, our only surviving victim. She is not ready but her memory is starting to return if we charge him now and he walks not only will she be in danger but we will not be able to charge him if she does regain her full memory," Carr is determined to do two things both get this guy and protect Nicole.

Everyone in the room sits quietly concentrating and thinking about what Agent Carr has said. They all know that she is probably right but they also know that without the charges for Nicole they cannot enter the drawing or memory of the truck or the witnesses that led them to him. They would only be left with the agents finding him at the scene of the latest victim. Fisher is the first to speak up.

"I know it may seem a little bit like abusing the system but I say we charge only for the first few victims before my team took over the case and the last victim. That means we can tie him up in court for a time while building a case for the others."

"The only problem with that is that the previous victims establish our contact with the case, our profiling, and a series of repetitive action that is how we were able to locate and determine who we were looking for," Rydell is analyzing in her mind what she needs and does not need to proceed.

"I know but right now we need to buy time and not let this guy go," Carr adds.

"I will have to see how far I can get with the judge he may let him off right away for lack of evidence if we try to go that route," Rydell explains.

The group adjourns and they all head their separate directions. Rydell heads to the office to make some calls and Fisher and Carr head back to the office to strategize. While they are driving back they discuss how attached Carr has become to this case. Fisher is worried about her and how she will react if the suspect gets to walk. He approaches the subject lightly hoping to receive an honest and quiet response. He does not want to bait her or make her feel like she is being attacked. He is truly concerned for her, not only as her boss but also as a friend. He has never seen her get so emotionally involved in a case and is now asking himself why he did not make her move on to another case.

"Are you going to be able to let go of your ties to this case if the judge lets him walk?" Fish asks.

"We can't let that happen," Carr mumbles.

"We may not have a choice besides we did our job and now it is out of our hands."

"And you are ok with that?" Carr looks Fisher in the eye waiting for an answer.

"It does not matter what I am ok with or not ok with this is my job and I did it the best I could."

"So we should tell Nicole that we earned our paycheck and beyond that she is on her own to deal with this creep getting away?" Carr is showing her agitation and does not seem to care.

"You need to step back and realize you are too emotionally involved in this case," Fisher leaves the statement lingering in the air.

"How can any human not be? I do my job and I try to stay separate but I stayed at this victims side and told her that if she tried to confront the demons inside her that this killer put there that we would lock him up and not let him do it again. We have him and I have to tell her that we may not have enough evidence and he may get to use a get out of jail free card."

"I understand but all we can do is our jobs, maybe we missed something somewhere. You are welcome to take a couple lab guys and go over the areas and clues we have again," Fisher can feel how much this case means to Carr so he eases up and offers his help.

"Thanks I may do just that. Will you keep me informed of what happens here?"

"Of course," Fisher says as he opens the door to his office and nods goodbye to Agent Carr.

Meanwhile, Rydell has been on the phone with every judge she knows trying to get an extension on the preliminary hearing for the case. She hangs up the phone after the last call with a bad taste in her mouth the longest she could get was 24 hours. She knew she was rolling the dice with this case and she had to hope that if nothing else she could get herself a trial date. She started to prep and assigned her assistant numerous tasks to complete. She works through the middle of the night with cold take-out food and so tired that her vision begins to blur. She works like this up until two hours before court when she has to run home to change and get to the courthouse. She hands off every piece of material she may need and sends her assistant to the courthouse with it. She gets into the elevator to take her to the garage and her car and leans her head against the wall with a sigh.

It is twenty minutes until court and Rydell walks up to the door with her fingers crossed behind her back, she hates stepping into a courtroom without every "t" crossed and "i" dotted. She surveys the room to see who all is in attendance and is surprised not to see Agent Rhonda Carr. She pays it no mind though and proceeds to her chair and waits for the judge.

Rydell presents everything she has to the judge trying to make it sound like more than it is. She gets a lot of resistance from the defense, more than she expected when she first saw the young attorney. The judge is not giving away his thoughts in his expression and this makes it even harder for Rydell to know how far to push her side onto the judge. She does not want to push too far causing the judge to become frustrated but she also does not want to stop short of convincing him either. She finishes up and so does the defense and the judge calls for a 30 minute recess. At this point Rydell is completely unsure of what the judge will say.

The judge returns with bad news for Rydell. His ruling comes quick and not as a surprise. He rules insufficient evidence to proceed with prosecution and orders the defendant released. The room falls quiet and Seamus sits back with an eerie smile sliding across his face. Rydell leaves in a hurry followed shortly by Agent Fishers quick steps.

"You tried. We will keep surveillance on him," Fisher offers Rydells back.

Rydell stops and turns to Fisher, "keep a car on him and get me something I can use. Where is Agent Carr and where are we at with the surviving victim?"

"She is out trying to get you what you need and I will keep in constant contact with you about anything we find."

"Ok." Rydell storms off unhappy and Fisher holds back letting her leave. Then he calls Agent Carr to give her the news that Seamus will be out on the streets in the next few hours.

CHAPTER TWENTY-SEVEN
The Release

———— ◊ ————

A few hours later Seamus is walking out onto the sidewalk next to the jail where they have been holding him. They released his clothes and personal items to him although they were not much. He smiles but knows he is hungry and tired and must start teaching again soon. He takes a few steps and is approached by an outstretched hand, he looks up at his attorney and takes his hand but only briefly enough to acknowledge the original act.

"Well, I have already received interested calls for your story."

"What do you mean?" Seamus asks knowing the answer.

"They want to produce your story into a movie or book. How can I keep in touch with you?"

"You can't. I will contact you if I am interested."

"But this could mean a lot of money ... wrongly accused plastered on the TV as a serial killer ... they owe you."

"They don't owe me. Now if you will excuse me I have work to do," Seamus smirks and moves past the attorney.

Seamus comes to realize very quickly that he is not alone like he is used to. His face is well known and some people stare. Others look away quickly as if by not seeing him that means that he is not there. They all could use a lesson or two. He does not like that he is no longer invisible he wants to continue his work and be left alone. He knows he will go down in history for his teachings and that he will be loved but he also knows right now is not that time. Right now he must continue his teachings and performing his work and eventually the world will understand and thank him. Until then he needs to keep a low profile which will be more difficult given the recent developments.

Seamus needs to take his mind off of the difficulties he faces and devise his plan for his next student before he is far too weak to proceed with it. He thinks about new areas to travel and how to become unnoticed since he is sure he will be followed by police. His mind drifts back to Nicole. They did not talk about Nicole in the hearing and he wonders why. She is a student who did not complete her lesson and he feels it may be more important to finish Nicole's lesson than to move on right now. He hashes it over in his head and quickly decides that Nicole must learn the rest of her lesson. He knows it will be hard to stay in the area and under the radar but perhaps he can trick them into thinking he left, send them on a wild goose chase while he quickly finishes his work.

First things first he will have to change his appearance a bit, hair cut and dye, different style clothes, a hat and maybe a tanning booth and some contacts. He decides these are all good ideas and heads towards the next city to start making changes, he will complete a circle, making one new change in each new area until he returns to Nicole. He will pay someone to drive his car out of town with a hat and hood on and only driving at night. He will need a busy place to find this person and make the switch. He walks by many places but as evening comes he decides the movie theatre would be the best place, dark and filled with people. It must be the place to be in this town he thought.

He watched a few movies before deciding on a young man that looked quite down on his luck, he sat behind him a row or two and watched as the young man went to sleep. He thought to himself that this guy must be homeless. He must have used whatever money he had to buy the movie ticket in order to have a warm place to sleep where the local police will not shoo him away.

After a while Seamus surveyed the surrounding people making sure they were into the film and not watching him and then moved to the seat directly behind the transient. He lightly poked the man on the shoulder and when he finally awoke he whispered in his ear not to turn around. He made his offer to the guy and held the money over his shoulder. The guy happily nodded yes and took the money and keys waiting out the rest of the movie before creeping out of the theatre just as Seamus asked. Seamus made sure to hand off the new ball cap he purchased that day and his zip up hoodie so that there would seem a resemblance to anyone watching. Seamus then headed to the restroom where he got himself ready. Once he heard noise in the halls he knew a different movie had just gotten out so he filed into the crowd but only long enough to sneak out an emergency exit. Once outside he pulled his jacket up and around his ears and started walking through the dark behind the theatre. He was happy with the arrangement he came to and even though the hole in his stomach was growing as he became more and more hungry he continued to stride forward content that he would be able to eat soon.

In the next 48 hours Seamus was able to get an old vehicle from a salvage yard in the next town over and successfully change his appearance. He was heading back to Nicole happy with his progress but losing the last bit of strength he had. Once he sees her he will be able to eat a little something to keep him going so that he can finish the lesson.

While he is driving back into town the officers tasked with following him were miles away watching his old parked car sit in a parking lot while the transient was able to sleep the day away until it was time to drive again throughout the night. One of the officers is growing impatient and tells his partner he is going to the vehicle to check things out because he is tired and sick of this routine. He exits the unmarked car they are sitting in and walks over to the other car, it is only minutes later that he is running back to the car shouting to his partner that they were fooled. It is already too late though since they have no idea when the switch was made. They can start a hunt for Seamus but no one would know what to look for or where to look. The FBI was notified and Agent Fisher called a small meeting to tell his team of these developments.

"So the idiots following our suspect lost him..." Fisher trailed off sounding angry.

"When did they lose him? Can we find him?" Agent Carr asked with agitation in her voice.

"They don't know."

"You can't be serious."

"So what now?" Agent Dalton asks.

"I don't know he could be anywhere by now," Fisher answers.

"I don't think so," Carr starts.

"You got an idea of where to look?" Agent Burke asks pushing Carr to continue.

"I think he made a mistake with Nicole and I think he knows it. I believe he will try to get to Nicole and tie up that loose end."

"But he has moved on before are we not sure that he is not just in the wind and hunting again?" Agent Vickers points out.

"He seems in a way smarter than that ... I suspect he realized that Nicole was not listed in the proceedings for a reason and he will be curious as to why that is and maybe paranoid enough to go after her," Carr states growing move confident in her belief.

"So what now?" Dalton repeats to Fisher.

"Well, it has come down to me that with the suspect gone we are to move on to other cases until something new resurfaces on this one," Fisher says slowly while looking at the floor.

"We are going to walk away from this case that has so much publicity, how will that look?" Burke wonders.

"Like we are cutting our losses and handing the case back to the local departments to handle."

"You mean walk away with our tail between our legs as if we were wrong?" Dalton snarls.

"Someone has to take the fall in the eyes of the press and this way the case can continue here for Nicole," Fisher looks to Carr.

"I want permission to stay behind and work with

Nicole and ..." Carr is trying to carefully pick her words.

"If you stay it is on your own time," Fisher is not directly answering Carr.

"Alright then I will," Carr answers and Fisher nods.

The team leaves the room to pack and head back home and Carr and Fisher talk for a few minutes more. Fisher understands why Carr wants to stay but still feels obligated to warn her about her emotions getting too involved in the case. Carr reminds him that she is a good agent because she cares so much about the cases that they work. He leaves her with a simple "just be careful".

While Carr moves her things to a cheap motel room and contemplates her next move Seamus has already started his. He has made his circle of cities and changed his appearance. He feels he is ready to teach again but is so hungry he is afraid that he will be unable to sufficiently complete a lesson. He must have something to eat soon, enjoyed or not he must find a way to be able to force something down. He wanders the streets during the afternoon keeping to himself but trying to find someone that he can take, teach, and rebuild his strength from. He looks and looks but realizes that no matter how hard he looks he cannot make himself settle for someone other than Nicole. He heads to her house to watch for her and see if he can catch a glimpse that may allow him some satisfaction.

Nicole was released from the hospital during the time

of the preliminary trial and had been taken home by her parents. They were worried that coming home may upset her instead of make her feel safer. They were right to worry, on the way home Nicole had a hard time dealing with the drive. She did not like being in the car or looking out the window at the neighborhood that seemed so familiar and so far away at the same time. Her last ride down this street was when she was taken and she was having a little trouble processing the scenery around her.

"How are you doing honey?" Her dad asked as he saw her eyes fill with tears as they drove towards home.

"Ok," she choked out.

"You know we will be home in just a minute but if it helps you could just lay down in the seat and relax till we get there," her mom offered picking up on her husbands cue.

"I would but I want to feel normal again and I can't do that if I am always hiding," Nicole responds feeling a little stronger just by saying the words.

"Ok, but sometimes it is okay to hide," her father offers with a proud smile on his face.

"Yeah hun, if you feel you need to don't deny yourself how you feel," her mother adds not knowing how else to ease her daughters pain.

"Really, I want to face this and soon we will be home which will feel weird but I am hoping nice. I spent a lot of time thinking about my room and I look forward to seeing it again."

"It will be nice to have you home again."

"Yes, it will but don't forget we are still available to help," her dad says winking at her in the rearview mirror.

It was only a short time later that they pulled into the drive way and were getting Nicole out of the car. She still needed a wheel chair but was able to walk herself with the assistance of crutches that attached to her lower arms from time to time. This was one of those times, she insisted on walking into the house instead of being pushed in a wheel chair. Although she wobbled and had trouble with the driveway she made it to the door with two teary-eyed parents following behind her. She got into the house and went straight to the sofa closest to the door and sat down. Her father pulled the wheel chair up to her and offered it without saying a word but she shook her head no. She gathered herself and started to make her way up the stairs, it was difficult and looked painful but she made it to her own room and sat upon her bed. Again her parents were just behind her following her as if she was a toddler learning to walk for the first time and may get hurt if she fell. They stood in her doorway proud of their daughter as Nicole held her head high and surveyed the room she had missed.

Once her parents finally left Nicole laid down on the bed staring at the ceiling. She was not completely void of thought and yet she had no complete thoughts running through her head. She admittedly felt safe in her room like she was untouchable there. Her room was her own tower, like a princess locked away from harm. She had to snicker and smile at the thought of herself in a tower with long hair running down the side of brick from the little window she would have, just like Rapunzel. She zoned out and little thoughts swirled in her mind not connecting until she fell to sleep. In her own bed in her own room she fell into the best, most comfortable sleep she could have imagined missing.

It was less than a week later that brought Seamus across the street from Nicole's home. Nicole had only left once for a physical therapy appointment and spent the rest of her time in her room trying to complete works of art through the frustration of relearning her own movements. Agent Carr had come to visit and Nicole felt obligated to remember more and frustrated that she could not. She thought that through her art she may be able to find the key to remembering.

Chapter Twenty-Eight
The Hunt

———————— ◊ ————————

S eamus watched the house for a few days unable to catch a glimpse of Nicole until her parents escorted her out to the physical therapist. He quickly decided to use this opportunity to find a way into and around the house. He was learning as he went since he usually did not take people from their homes. Then again in his mind he had already come to realize that Nicole was not part of the norm. He found himself becoming obsessed with her unable to let the idea go that he had to have her he had to be able to finish teaching her. She was the one student he had failed with and he could not let that be. He believed that every student was teachable if he just made the extra effort.

He moved around the house looking for ways in

and found several. He could enter through a window or through the sliding door. He chose the sliding door he simply pushed in on the glass until it pulled far enough from the frame that he could lift the lock with his pocket knife. Once inside he began a mental painting that would become his map of this house. He went into every room counting his steps and tracing every object into his mind. He knew he would have to enter when everyone was asleep and that the house would be dark and he would need to be able to move throughout the house without any disruption. The plan was to be in and out as quickly as possible with the girl in tow. He would need to get something to knock her out, perhaps a chemical so that she did not make a sound. He went through the house a few times and then exited the same way he entered even using his knife to re-latch the lock.

Nicole and her parents returned to the house having no idea that anyone else had been inside their home. Nicole settled into the living room knowing that her friends would be coming by. First Jill arrived and filled Nicole in on the gossip around town. Ryan arrived a little later hoping that Jill would leave soon so that he could have time with Nicole alone.

"Hey Jill, been here long?" Ryan says looking at Jill.

"Not really, just catching Nicole up on things."

"That sounds fun …"

"I was just telling her about some of the new clicks at school and how Justin is seeing everyone but Alicia,"

Jill trails off wondering if she should talk about Justin in front of Ryan knowing that Ryan likes Nicole.

"I see. So, how are you and Cameron doing?"

"We've been better and he can drive me crazy but we are good," Jill seems to be babbling.

"What does that mean?" Nicole started to pry.

"You know ... he is never around and I miss him at school and then we fight about not having time together and even fight about fighting when we are together."

"That sounds like too much fighting," Ryan interrupts.

"He is right ... if you are not happy you should end it while you can still be friends," Nicole adds.

"We talked about it and we do not want to end it we just want to make it through the year and then we will both be out of school and looking forward together," Jill says looking away unsure if she believes what she is telling her best friend.

"I will support whatever you decide but I hope you know that we all want you to be happy."

"That's true," Ryan says thinking to himself that he really wants her to be happy but right now he really just wants her to leave.

"Well, I should head out. Lots to do," Jill stands up as if reading Ryan's mind.

"Ok, I will talk to you later," Nicole says making herself stand to give Jillian a hug goodbye.

"Sure, I will call you tonight."

"So, the legs seem strong today," Ryan motions to Nicole's legs as she reseats herself on the sofa.

"I had a good session, they said before I know it my strength will be back and I will be running around," Nicole says with a half smile.

"That's great, why don't you seem more happy?"

"I just get sick of hearing how it will be so soon but when I ask the doctor he warns me that to feel fully normal again like walking and such is probably still a year away."

"Yeah, but throughout the year you will be improving it won't be one way now and then a whole new you when you wake up a year from today," Ryan reassured her.

"I know ... I just feel... I want to be better already ... to feel strong again."

"I know. How is the art coming any less frustrating?"

"Yeah, actually even when I am frustrated I feel like myself again when I am painting. The finished product is not as good but it feels like it is mine and represents me. At first I hated them and kept throwing them out then I realized that the art would never look the same because it is not the same person doing it. It will not be my life's work now but I will always have it to make me happy. Plus, the tutor they assigned to catch me up seems to think my brain is worth something too," Nicole roles her eyes jokingly.

"Really, there is actually a brain in there. I must of

missed that discovery," Ryan jokes back peering at the top of Nicole's head.

Nicole reaches over to push on Ryan's arm and say "hey" and as she is pulling her hand back he slides his hand down her forearm to lock her hand into his own. He gazes at her while holding her hand for a moment before speaking. They are staring into each other eyes and this is the first time that Nicole has not instinctively pulled her hand away. She is getting more comfortable with Ryan and herself. What disgusted and embarrassed her before about her damaged and partial fingers no longer held such a high importance to her and she believed that they did not bother Ryan either.

"Why don't we have a night out? Maybe see a new movie? You have not been to the movies in a long time and it has to be getting stuffy in this house all the time," Ryan waits watching her face for a response.

"I am not sure I am ready for that yet. I don't know how I will feel about seeing people and answering questions and I am afraid of the looks and whispers," Nicole trails off starting to pull her hand away but Ryan is determined and holds her had tighter and leans into her.

"Forget everyone else. One of the things I love about you Nicole is your ability to be who you are and fight when many others would have written off the world and given up. You went through a horrible thing and came out on the other side yourself, the wonderful, charismatic, beautiful Nicole that you were before. You are stronger than you realize and everyone else does not matter. I will wait if that is what you decide but I want to be with you when you decide that it is time to face that part of life again." Before Nicole can respond Ryan tenderly touches his lips to hers. It is a timid kiss but one that sparks a fire in Nicole.

"I forget sometimes that you were not in my life before and wonder what I ever did without you. Of course there is no one else I would rather go out with than you," she leans forward and kisses him again, amazed at how easy it is.

Nicole and Ryan spent the rest of the evening talking and laughing. Ryan even tried to do some drawing with Nicole that came out pretty funny. Nicole forgot for a while that she was different now and she felt like she used to. She also felt beautiful which she knew was because of Ryan. She had been so scared to let him or anyone else touch her but for some reason she felt safe now with him. She thought to herself that maybe all she needed was to be at home. She remained scared about going out into town but worked it out with her parents and Ryan and was determined to try, no matter how hard it would be. She felt it was the least she could do for Ryan considering how wonderful he has been to her despite what happened to her.

Ryan felt excited about the opportunity to take Nicole out and really thought it would help her to move on. He knew she was fighting to remember everything that happened to her and he felt it may be better to move past it than to try to release those things her mind had shut away. He thought that by going out she would see that there were things to do that she did not even realize she was missing. In no time she would be focused on other things. Of course, one of those things he was hoping would be him. He was not sure if Nicole would have ever liked him before the incident and he was unsure if she would continue to like him after she realized other guys will still want to be with her. At this point he did not care, he hoped to continue to build a relationship with Nicole but if she needed someone else he would try to understand and remain her friend. He knew he was in love with her and wanted nothing but happiness for her.

It was a few nights later that Ryan arrived to pick up Nicole, she insisted on riding in his car and not taking the wheel chair. She told her parents that at the movies or getting dinner she would be sitting and she was determined to walk from place to place she was not having everyone see her in a wheel chair her first time out. They would all have to look down on her in a wheelchair and that would make it harder. Ryan reassured her parents that he would not let her push herself too far and that he would be there to help the whole time. Her parents reluctantly gave in with worried looks on their faces and tears showing in the corners of her mother's eyes. Nicole used her canes that attached at her elbows and felt a little more dignified at least being able to stand and look others in the eyes.

Ryan helped Nicole into the car and headed to his side reminding Nicole's parents that they could reach them on his cell phone as well as Nicole's. After a minute they drove away from the house.

"How you doing over there? You look very nice tonight," Ryan says testing the waters.

"I am happier than I thought I would be to be out of the house. I have butterflies in my stomach though."

"Don't worry I will not leave your side."

"I know you won't," Nicole smiles over at Ryan remembering the kiss a few nights before and wondering when and if he will kiss her again. She feels silly but likes feeling silly again.

"So what kind of movie are you thinking?" Ryan asks smiling back.

"No horror, please. How about a comedy?" Nicole answers.

"We think the same, there is a romantic comedy playing that I think you would like."

"Ok, that sounds good. I am glad you talked me into this," Nicole says watching Ryan as he drives.

"I thought you talked me into it," Ryan answers with a laugh.

"Yeah, right."

"I am glad you decided to come out too," he says reaching over and placing his hand atop hers.

They rode for a bit in silence holding hands and enjoying the idea of being out together alone. They were used to having her parents or nurses or Jillian always around, they both liked how together they felt and that no one was there to interrupt it. However, what they did not know was that Seamus was only a little ways behind them, following everywhere they went. Seamus was surprised to see Nicole out of the house and he felt angry that he let her go long enough to hurt this guy. He would make sure that the lesson stuck this time. He waited while they watched the movie and waited while they ate a burger place with a bunch of friends. He watched every move that Nicole made. At the end of the night he followed them back to her house, parking and watching from down the street.

At the door Nicole and Ryan were saying goodnight with no idea that Seamus was watching them. They kissed passionately outside before Ryan helped Nicole inside. Once inside Ryan left Nicole to travel the stairs herself and said goodnight to the waiting parents who looked relieved to have their daughter home again. A few minutes later Ryan was driving down the street away from Nicole's house. Seamus watched the house for lights and waited until every last one was out. He knew it had to be tonight.

Seamus entered the house in the middle of the night recounting the same steps he had taken just a couple days before. He found his way slowly through the house making sure not to be heard and that he heard nothing. He made his way up the stairs and heard the father snoring reassuring him that he was asleep. Once at Nicole's door he pulled the rag out of his left pocket and the small bottle out of his right, he poured the chloroform onto the rag and slowly turned the knob on the door. He walked in and to the bed placing the rag over Nicole's mouth quickly and calmly. Nicole awoke and reached for the rag over her mouth but she only had a moment before the chemical took effect and she was out. Seamus picked up her body in his arms placing the rag back into his pocket and began carrying her out of the house retracing the same steps he used to enter the house. He placed her in his car and drove away.

Seamus felt a little nostalgic and against his own better judgment took Nicole back to the same housing development he had used before. The house that he originally used was finished but there was a new phase started and plenty to choose from. He took her to where he had set things up thinking to himself how much faster this one could be to avoid being interrupted again and because she already had the first half of the lesson. He removed her clothes and tied her up. He then left to get some supplies like food and such since he would finally be able to enjoy it and wanted to be sure that he did before he finished her since it would go much faster this time.

CHAPTER TWENTY-NINE
Missing

———————— ◊ ————————

Agent Carr continued her search for Seamus and the evidence needed to lock him up on, she felt as if she was hitting a brick wall. A couple nights before Nicole was taken however there was a tip and a discovery. The department had found Seamus' truck, or at least what they thought was his truck. The investigators had it sent to them at their lab where they would start to dissect it and try to tie it to Seamus or even some of the girls. Carr was feeling lucky considering the tip was anonymous and actually proved to be a valuable tip. She was anxious to tell Nicole they had found something but so far all they had was the truck and no proof it was the one they wanted, but Carr had a feeling in her gut that it was Seamus' truck and that they would find something.

A couple days later and Agent Carr's gut was proven correct. The rushed report was released to Carr per Fishers instructions and she felt excited as she read what she needed to link the truck to both Seamus and Nicole. Seamus had fingerprints on the underside of the steering wheel somewhere he had not reached with bleach. There was also a blood spot that had been washed away right above the glove box, but gave them a place to start looking. They luckily found a hair that was stuck in the keyhole of the glove box. At first it seemed a waste since the strand of hair had been drowned in bleach but on a whim they decided to take apart the lock and carefully they did, finding an end of hair that had remained untouched by bleach. It took 24 hours to run the test but they were able to match the DNA in the hair to Nicole. So with the report in hand Agent Carr headed to Nicole's house to fill her in.

Agent Carr did not even realize how early it was when she pulled up to Nicole's house, the yard was still damp with dew and the cars in the driveway were still iced over. It was early but Carr did not want to wait. She knocked on the door and Nicole's father answered a little bewildered either by the early visitor or just because it was early, Carr could not tell. He stood there for a moment just looking at her before Carr asked if she could come in and with an embarrassed look motioned his head to the side saying come in. They went towards the kitchen where Nicole's mother was and Carr could smell the coffee was brewing.

Each of them made a cup of coffee before Carr asked about Nicole.

"So, what time does Nicole usually get out of bed?"

"It really depends …before she would sleep all day if you let her but now," Nicole's mom trailed off, leaving her dad to finish the statement.

"She is usually up early but she does not always come down, sometimes she just stays in her room and paints."

"Do you know if she is up already?" Carr hints.

"I am not sure but I can check," Nicole's dad starts to head towards the stairs.

"Is everything ok?" Her mom asks timidly.

"Sure…good even," Carr leaves it hanging in the air.

"You know, she went out last night for the first time. I mean without us with a boy and all, she seemed to really…" Nicole's mom is interrupted by her father.

"She's not here!" He is shouting over and over as he comes running down the stairs.

"What do you mean?"Carr asks a little confused, Nicole's mother is already bawling.

"She is not in her room, the bathroom, any room upstairs or down. She is not here!"

"Any chance she did not come home from her night out?" Carr is hoping.

"No. We watched her climb the stairs and she said good night smiling and her bed has been used," he is starting to ramble.

Carr pulls out her cell phone and starts making calls

it is only a matter of 5 to 10 minutes before the local police and the crime scene team are there but to Nicole's parents it feels like a lifetime. Carr wants to get them relaxed so that she can get some answers from them so she takes them into the living room and sets them down on the couch.

"So what time did she come back and who was she with last night?"

"She was in around eleven not late and she was with the boy Ryan, you know him," Nicole's father has to answer the questions because her mother is sobbing into his shoulder unable to talk.

"Yes, let's call Ryan over and see what he knows."

"Sure his cell number is on the fridge."

"Ok, and where did they go?" Agent Carr motions with her head for the officer in the room to get the number and make the call so she can stay focused on the parents.

"Movies and that burger place the kids hang out at."

"Ok, when did you two go to bed?"

"It was a while after she got home. We were talking about her moving on and letting her do it and…"

"Did you lock up before going to bed?"

"Yeah. We locked the front door right after Nicole got home."

"Ok," Carr was looking down thinking.

"Do you think it's him?" Nicole's mother lifts her head and stammers.

"I am not sure what to think yet. Let me go see what I can find out and I will be back in a minute," she says patting the mother's knee as she stands up.

Agent Carr talks to all the leads in the house to get an update. The most helpful being the crime scene investigators who had already determined a struggle in the bedroom and how the person got into the house. They showed her the markings on the lock of the sliding door from the pocket knife and that the door had not been completely locked down. Agent Carr now thought for sure that this was not random and that Seamus had to be involved. She went back to the parents and assured them everything will be fine and started to leave as Ryan walked in.

"Hello Ryan, I am sorry to call you over so early."

"What's happening? Is Nicole ok? The police guy on the phone would not tell me anything and the guys outside just pointed me in here…is Nicole ok?"

"Well, why don't you sit down and we will talk about it?" Carr motions toward the couch.

"Ok," he settles into a seat not too far from the parents, watching them cry he knows something is wrong.

"Nicole is missing." Carr watches for Ryan's response.

"What do you mean missing? I saw her last night she was here…"

"I know. That is one reason I wanted to talk to you.

Did you notice anyone different last night that hung around you two or maybe watched Nicole?"

"Well, no one strange a lot of people we don't usually talk to or some we did not know recognized Nicole and came by to say hi but no one strange."

"No one looked at Nicole funny or …"

"You mean the guy from before? That guy you tried to catch and they let go?"

"Maybe," Carr could not finish the statement as both parents shot to attention with concern.

"We need to keep positive and think constructively. Anything you can think of may help. Let me know and I will have the officer continue to canvas the area for anything any neighbor may have seen and I will leave a patrol officer here to watch the house," Carr starts to walk away but Ryan stands and follows her out the front door.

"Hey, Agent Carr."

"Yes, Ryan? I told you, you can call me Rhonda."

"Ok Rhonda, be honest with me if it is the same guy why did he not just kill her here? Why take her with him."

"I think you are a smart guy Ryan and you know why."

"Because he sticks to his routine?"

"Something like that, his mind does not work like yours or mine he may want to finish what he started but he may think he has to start over to do that."

"So where can you find him?"

"I am not sure. He could be anywhere."

"Last time it was a house right?"

"Yes, but he uses many abandoned places we will find her don't worry," Carr says as she walks away unsure of her belief in her own statement.

Ryan stood on the lawn for a minute thinking before he ran to his car and started home. He had only one thing on his mind, finding Nicole and protecting her from the psycho trying to hurt her. He was recalling all of the conversations and mumbled voices that he had eves dropped on since Nicole was found. He was trying to remember exactly where Nicole was found, what housing development. He had a gut feeling that the bastard that took Nicole would take her back there. If the guy was so determined to do things the same Ryan was sure the guy would take Nicole back there. He pulled up at his house and ran in, before even returning to his still running vehicle he remembered where they said they found Nicole and he headed in that direction, determined.

Agent Carr was not far behind Ryan in her line of thinking. She also had a funny feeling that although the killer was intelligent enough to evade all efforts to catch him so far that he would slip up like with the truck that he must have hastily discarded since it did not have his normal detailed cleaning. In her mind she analyzed it out and could not help but think that if Seamus took the chance to return and stay in the area instead of moving on then he probably felt himself linked to Nicole and felt he had to finish what he started. If he felt he was finishing it instead of just removing the lose end then he may even believe that he has to finish it in the same place as it started. She called in for the directions from her location to the site where Nicole was found. It took a few minutes but she received the address plugged it into her GPS just in case and started heading to the location hoping to find Nicole before it was too late.

Meanwhile, Nicole is still unconscious and Seamus is just returning to watch her body shake and shiver in the cold and enjoy his sandwich. He had to go further away to shop for supplies to be sure he was not seen close by or recognized. He watched for hours waiting for her to awake on her own, wanting her to wake on her own. He anticipated the lessons to teach once she awakes and he hummed and whispered "don't worry I will teach you well."

CHAPTER THIRTY
The Last Victim

———— ◊ ————

Nicole starts to open her eyes but they are so heavy she wonders if they are taped shut. It takes a couple minutes before the fog starts to clear and her vision begins to return. She does not realize it but she is groaning and whining. Seamus is enjoying the noises she is making and waits knowing it will take a while for her to feel awake and be able to see around her or understand what is happening. He watches in anticipation. Nicole continues to squirm and moan.

After a few minutes have past Nicole is able to focus enough to see Seamus sitting across the room on the hard floor. She recognizes the smell, the look and the texture of everything around her but is at first unsure of why. She is no longer making noise but simply watching Seamus waiting to see what he will do. She has the strangest feeling of déjà vu and knows this must be how it was before. At first she does not even recognize Seamus but as he begins to talk to her she realizes who it is.

"You did not finish your lesson before," Seamus starts out shaking his head back and forth.

"I felt as a good teacher I must take the time to finish teaching you before I left," he pauses between each sentence waiting for a response but she is not giving one.

"Oh, that's right you do not remember me or our lessons do you?" He smirks and stands to raise the cold hose over her naked body pouring salt over her at the same time.

"Stop. Stop. Stop," she yells and squirms.

"You must think I am a horrible teacher. My first lesson did not take but it is ok because I learned some new teaching techniques since we last saw each other," he says as he is wrapping a leather belt around his hand with the tail of it hanging down.

"Fuck you," is all that Nicole could muster up or even think to say.

"See you should have better manners. I am trying to help you and you are so unappreciative."

He pulls back his arm and wails it forward snapping the leather against Nicole's skin as she bites her lip. She is determined not to scream and bites down so hard that she draws blood. She looks up at him with flared nostrils and squinted eyes. She is angry more than she is scared and Seamus notices this.

"Do you remember me? Is that why you are mad or am I not doing it right?" He says taunting her while walking over to his supplies.

Without a word he pulls out a knife and returns to her side, this time she looks a little more frightened and that makes Seamus happy. He must have her in the right state of mind to learn her lessons. He takes the blade and tenderly touches her side at first sliding it down along her hip and onto her thigh making no marks. He pulls it back to the top and once he reaches the top of the thigh he begins to push the blade into her skin. Only a little at first the equivalent of a paper cut then slicing lower and lower as she begins to squeal in pain. He smiles at his work and lifts the blade to start again repeating it a few times before standing and walking back to the hose. He takes the hose and sprays her down making sure to dump extra salt on the open wounds on her leg. She thrashes back in forth in pain and in anger. He stops and begins to talk to her again.

"So as I was saying, we need to teach you some lessons."

"Go to hell," she says through clinched teeth glaring at Seamus.

"I see you think you know better than me. That is one of those problems that women like you have. You end up destroying so many people that way. I will teach you not to though. I wonder what ever happened to that boyfriend of yours," he trails off in his own thoughts.

"You are crazy and disgusting…"

At this Seamus gets down close to her face and looks her in the eyes and whispers, "No. I am the hero." While he looks into her eyes and makes this last statement a door in Nicole's mind springs open and memories start to surface. They are quite out of focus at first but within moments they are becoming clearer and they fuel her anger. She looks back at Seamus and unable to get loose or fight back she is left with one thing, her words.

"You will never be known as a hero! They won't even remember that your name is Seamus," she waits for a response.

"You remember my name or you saw it on TV?" He is looking at her with his head tilted to the side inquisitively.

"This is not the same house what happened you could not remember where you were before?" She says ignoring his question.

"This place is fine. Your lesson could be completed anywhere," he is getting visibly angry.

"Yeah, that's right you think you are helping people and saving them from me," she laughs a loud fake laugh hoping to drive the insult in further.

"You talk too much!" He starts to yell but quickly calms himself, "that is okay though I will develop a lesson for that as well. We will have to work quickly there are others that need my teachings."

"You know I would have recognized you sooner if you had not changed so much. I guess it was time for a make-over. That was probably a good idea but I am not sure it helped you any …"

"Let us begin your next lesson," He begins tightening the ropes and belts around her to see it start to cut into her skin and takes out his leather piece again. This time he aims at her face and she blacks out.

Seamus is glad that she is quiet now and feels even more rejuvenated in his belief that girls like Nicole need to be taught a lesson. Since he seems to be the only one with the courage and strength to do it, he is the hero. He continues playing with her like a doll. He is enjoying the marks that begin to form on her body and with every shiver she has he feels warmer. Every moan she makes helps him to smile. He is standing and cleaning, dumping bleach over the body and gaining amusement out of the noises Nicole is subconsciously making as the bleach pours into her still bleeding cuts. He stops and sits to watch for a while and finds himself able to doze off for the first good sleep since his last victim.

Nicole awakes and see Seamus asleep, she feels weak and sore. She begins to look around and imagine ways out of where she is. She tells herself there is no way that this guy will win. The more she tries to move though the more pain there is, and the more desperate she is starting to feel. Her mind seems to be working on two levels and yet they are overlapping and confusing her. On one side she is cataloging everything she see's around her and trying to plan a way out and on the other hand she is recalling the previous attack. She wonders now if others were right and she would have been better off with those memories tucked far away in her mind somewhere that she could not get to them. She thinks she hears some noise outside and tries to listen hard. Unfortunately, Seamus is up and moving toward her so his noise overshadows the noise outside.

Seamus begins talking again and tightening the ropes. He asks if she is hungry yet and if she is in pain. Faking concern he asks all the questions a mother or father would ask their child when checking on them however he wants the opposite response. He feels so alive and feels that with one more meal he may just have to end her himself. She is a strong one, hard to break. He is not going to let that stop him though.

"I think it is time to roll you over and start on the other side."

She is confused at first about what he means but it takes only moments before she realizes he is going to cut her again. She cannot remember any cuts from before but he did say he learned some new things. He begins to roll her over, her skin roughly passing over the paint pieces and cement chunks covering the wood flooring.

"I think I will be creative with this lesson," Seamus mused bent over Nicole knife in hand.

"Back off!" An exclamation comes from the doorway behind Seamus. Seamus had turned his back to it when he rolled Nicole over. In his anxiousness for the next lesson Seamus forgot to reposition himself on the other side of Nicole for his clear views of the entrances, exits, and the street. He turned slowly to see who was there and was surprised and delighted to see a boy, by himself.

"Can I help you with something?" Seamus teased.

"Get away from her!" Nicole recognizes the voice although she has never heard such anger or volume in it before.

"Well… I can't do that," Seamus responds with a smirk on his face and shaking his head.

"I said get away from her! NOW!" Ryan yells at Seamus unsure how to take his behavior.

"Like I said kid, I can't do that," Seamus is growing tired of this game and has determined he must kill the boy.

"Move away from her or I'll make you," Ryan snarls letting the words hang in the air as he pulls his hand from his pocket and points the gun at Seamus.

"I would not do that," Seamus smirks and slides the knife to Nicole's throat.

"Just give it up. Let her go!" The more Ryan tries to sound strong the more his own nervousness shows through.

"Have you ever used a gun?" Seamus asks baiting the boy.

"Yes. Now move away from Nicole."

"You must be the boyfriend? Although I have yet to figure out if you are the one from before or the new one. It doesn't matter I will save you anyways, even if you are causing me problems."

"Shut up and move away from her."

"Make me," Seamus is teasing Ryan and giving himself time to plan.

Seamus figures he can get close enough to take the gun away or wound him with the knife then take the gun and dispose of the boy. He wants to do this quickly because he realizes if this guy could find him so could others but he does not want to be hasty in finishing Nicole. He continues to poke at Ryan getting him to come closer with every threat to Nicole. His plan is taking longer than he likes but it is working.

Once Ryan is close enough Seamus lunges forward with the knife at Ryan but before making contact there are two gunshots and Seamus' body slumps to the ground. Ryan drops his gun instantly and stands stunned for a moment. From the other side of the house through a window opening Agent Carr stands with her weapon pointed in Ryan's direction. It takes but a moment of them looking at each other and Ryan is bent at Nicole's side and Agent Carr is rounding the house to enter.

"Nicole. I am here, Nicole," Ryan says as he crouches at her back.

"I know," is all Nicole can say looking up at him with streams of tears running down her face.

"I'm going to get you outta here."

"I know."

Ryan begins removing the ropes as the sounds of sirens arrive outside. Agent Carr is checking on Seamus and removing weapons from the area just in case. She is worried about Ryan. He should not have been there and not with a gun and she hoped it was her bullet that went through Seamus and not Ryan's. He would have to go through so much in paperwork and formalities and she just wanted Nicole and everyone else around her to be able to move past this.

"Are you both ok?" Carr reaches down and drapes her long jacket over Nicole as Ryan finishes removing the ropes at her feet.

"I remember," Nicole stammers looking up at Agent Carr.

"I'm sorry sweetie."

"I can help now. I remember," Nicole answers.

"She's a little out of it," Ryan offers.

"You should not have been here Ryan," Carr says looking over at him.

"I had to."

"You could have been hurt or killed."

"I had to."

"And the gun? Where did you get the gun?"

"My dad's. Did I?"

"I did. You don't worry about anything. You did the best thing for Nicole. You were here for her."

"But I," Ryan let this trail off not really wanting the answer and hoping Agent Carr was right and that he did not kill the man laying on the floor but that she did.

"Agent Carr," an officer is waving at Carr to come over to him. He is standing over the gurney supporting Seamus' body.

"Yes, what is it?"

"He is alive."

"What?"

"He is still alive. He has two gunshot wounds but one is in his foot and the other his chest. We will know more at the hospital but the paramedics tell me he has a pulse and they are rushing him in."

"Thank you. And for the girl?" Agent Carr motions towards Nicole asking when she will be taken.

"There is a second team here waiting for your go ahead to take her."

"Alright, go ahead."

Agent Carr returns to Nicole's side unsure of what information to divulge and what to keep to herself. Nicole is already more awake and aware than a few moments before. Nicole is asking for cloths or a blanket embarrassed about being naked in front of so many strange people. Every time the paramedics try to touch her she pushes them away.

"Honey, you have to let them help you," Agent Carr offers.

"I'm fine," she states with a quivering lip.

"Honey…"

"No. I will go on my own," Nicole sounds determined but they all see that she can barely push herself up.

"Nicole, let me help," Ryan says offering his hand out to her to take if she wishes.

"Where is he?" Nicole asks looking around.

"Who?" Agent Carr asks knowing the answer.

"Seamus."

"Gone. You are going to be fine."

"Dead?" Nicole asks showing no emotion on her face.

Agent Carr and Ryan both answer at the same time. Ryan responds, "yes," and Agent Carr responds "not exactly."

"What?" Ryan and Nicole say in unison.

"He may die on the way to the hospital or at the hospital but he is still alive so far," Agent Carr tells them maneuvering herself over to Nicole's side.

"If he lives …" Ryan lets the question hang in the air.

"If he lives, he is going away for the rest of his life."

"Rhonda, I remember," Nicole adds staring blankly at Agent Carr.

"I know sweetie and he will never come close to you again."

"Ok," Nicole reaches towards Ryan for help up.

Ryan and Agent Carr together begin to raise Nicole up and as they do the paramedics are telling them to stop and put her down. Everyone is looking around frantically but they set her down and the medics move in.

"What?" Agent Carr asks.

"You can't move her that way, she is losing too much blood."

"Why didn't you say that before?"

"We could not see how bad it was until you raised her off that leg. Let us bandage it up and we will gurney her and take her to the hospital and they can stitch it up for her."

"Alright. I will meet you at the hospital Nicole. I am going to get your parents they are very worried and we will see you at the hospital."

"But …" Nicole's thought is interrupted by a wince as the pain shoots through her body as they tightened the bandages around her leg.

"I will go with her and stay with her," Ryan says to Carr and Nicole, he has tears in the corners of his eyes having to watch Nicole in so much pain.

"Thank you," Agent Carr says and walks away. She is amazed at the strength of this young man and his determination to protect Nicole. It actually makes her feel like Nicole will always be safe now.

"Is that ok with you?" Ryan turns his gaze onto Nicole.

"Yes," is all Nicole says before her eyes begin to drop unable to fight the swelling that wants to shut them.

Ryan holds her hand all the way to the hospital and never stops watching her. At the hospital he is allowed to go in with her but once the doctors take over he is forced into the waiting room with Nicole's parents and Agent Carr. The doctor assures them that Nicole is going to be fine they just want to get her nourished and fixed up and then they can all go in and see her. Agent Carr walks towards the door phone in hand. Anytime she walks away like that it is usually important so Ryan decides to listen in as he has so many times before.

"Hey Fish, we have him."

"Great. Is he alive?" Agent Fisher asks.

"He is not stable and I don't know if he will make it," Agent Carr answers.

"And the girl, Nicole how is she?"

"She will be ok."

"Good. So we can lock him up or?" Fisher says as if he is waiting for the bad news.

"Yes. Nicole was his last victim. This guy is done. We have everything we need," Agent Carr offers.

"Great job. We will see you soon."

"Thanks Fish for letting me finish this one out."

"You earned it."

Agent Carr hangs up the phone and turns to see Ryan focused on her.

"Are you sure?" Ryan asks.

"Sure, what?"

"Sure you have everything you need and that he will never get out to come after Nicole or anyone else again?"

"Yes, I am more than sure Ryan."

"Ok," Ryan does not seem too relieved.

"Besides he has to live first and then he would have to get through you. You did a great job for Nicole."

"Thanks. I could not help but think that if we had not gone out …"

"No Ryan, he was watching the house at least a week before you went out, we talked to the neighbors. You have helped Nicole and you are going to have to start all over. I hope you can handle that," she is searching his face for answers.

"If Nicole can suffer like she has and be ok… the least I can do is try to help make it ok for her. I love her."

"I know you do and she is lucky to have you."

"I am lucky to have her. She makes you live life for the moment like no one I have ever met, even before the first attack."

"That is sweet."

"That is true. She is charismatic in a way that just thinking about the glow around her makes you smile. She is special and I just hope I can show that to her."

"I think you will do fine. It will be hard but you will make it through it. Tomorrow there will be a lot of tough questions and statements and such just call me if you need anything or just want someone here and tell Nicole the same," she turns to walk away.

"Rhonda, I think you are wrong," Ryan says.

"What do you mean?" Carr turns and looks at him.

"Nicole was not his last victim. She was the first one that refused to be a victim. She is a fighter and the first survivor. She is not "his last victim" she does not give him the satisfaction of living her life as his anything."

"I believe you are right," Agent Carr says and turns back towards the door and smiles thinking to herself how right Ryan is and how special Nicole is.

The parents turn to Ryan and nod approval at what he had said and begin to offer their own thoughts but are interrupted by the doctors. The doctors bring a good report and say they all can sit in the room with Nicole if they want. For now though they have to let her sleep but she should be up in a few hours to eat. They also tell them that she was asking for all of them the entire time, her parents and Ryan. Ryan smiles at this and Nicole's mom hugs him. They go into the room and sit down quietly waiting for Nicole to wake up. They are all eager to move on this time and determined to move on. They all want to be like Nicole, they want to be fighters, survivors. They will not let themselves become Seamus' last victim.

Printed in the United States
219371BV00001B/17/P